Absolute Forgiveness

Absolute Forgiveness

A Novel

Addison Paisley

iUniverse, Inc.
New York Lincoln Shanghai

Absolute Forgiveness

Copyright © 2008 by Addison Paisley

All rights reserved. No part of this book may be used or reproduced by any means, graphic, electronic, or mechanical, including photocopying, recording, taping or by any information storage retrieval system without the written permission of the publisher except in the case of brief quotations embodied in critical articles and reviews.

iUniverse books may be ordered through booksellers or by contacting:

iUniverse
2021 Pine Lake Road, Suite 100
Lincoln, NE 68512
www.iuniverse.com
1-800-Authors (1-800-288-4677)

Because of the dynamic nature of the Internet, any Web addresses or links contained in this book may have changed since publication and may no longer be valid.

This is a work of fiction. All of the characters, names, incidents, organizations, and dialogue in this novel are either the products of the author's imagination or are used fictitiously.

ISBN: 978-0-595-48667-0 (pbk)
ISBN: 978-0-595-60762-4 (ebk)

Printed in the United States of America

For "Girl"

Chapter 1

▼

Damn it! Not again! Andrea muttered as she passed the same gas station for the third time. She quickly glanced over at the digital clock on the dashboard of her rental car and acknowledged that it was too late to call the office for better directions.

I should have asked for a car with a GPS in it, she said to herself and then chuckled. *Not that it would have been helpful out here.* Except for the occasional run down shack and a gas station here or there, there wasn't much in the way of civilization around.

Accepting defeat, she quickly did a u-turn and headed back to the gas station she had just passed. Hopefully, someone there would know where the hell Parsley Lane was. Behind the counter stood a tall, gangly old man wearing worn out blue jeans and a white t-shirt. An old ball cap covered his mostly balding head and a lit cigarette hung loosely from his lips.

Not in Kansas anymore, she thought as she observed the man shuffling through the pages of what appeared to be a hunting magazine, completely oblivious to her.

"Excuse me," Andrea said tentatively, "I was wondering if you could help me, it seems I'm a bit lost."

"Whatcha lookin fer?" he asked without looking away from his magazine.

"Parsley Lane?" she replied, somewhat taken aback by his southern drawl. She had travelled to many parts of the world, and had covered most of the United States at one time or another, so she was well used to the diverse accents and each region's slightly different use of the English language. Somehow, she was still shocked to hear it. Maybe, it was because she had only travelled six hours by car away from her hometown in Ohio, and this was the first person she had come into contact with, that it had taken her by surprise.

He finally looked up from his magazine but didn't look at her. He simply looked out the window and pointed.

"Follar this here road North fer a spell 'till you get to the crick; then, make a right on the next black top road you come up on. There'll be an ole rusty shed on your left 'n Parsley Lane'll be on yur right." He paused for a moment, as if to decide if those directions were clear enough. "Aint much in the way of a road though," he added before directing his attention back to his magazine.

"Thanks," Andrea said as she made her way out of the tiny dilapidated building and back to her car. *Well, that was fun.*

At least his directions were accurate, she noted as she pulled into the gravel driveway of the split-level log cabin.

Hope my new roommates are a little more cordial, she thought as she took in the beautiful scenery for the first time.

Being very much a people-person, Andrea preferred to stay in rooming houses or at least apartments whenever her assignments lasted longer than a couple of weeks. Since this one was going to last the better part of six months, her client arranged for her to lease a room in this house for the duration of her stay. She was feeling a bit nervous about it, but looked forward to making new friends, something she could not do if she stayed in a hotel.

As a result of these types of accommodations, Andrea had made many good friends all over the country and she could always stay with them whenever she was in the neighbourhood. She cherished every friendship. Her friends were her only family.

Andrea had never worked in North Carolina before, so this would be a new experience for her. Judging from the exterior of the dwelling, it appeared to be clean and well kept. Her client had told her that there were two other women living there, one of which owned the property, the other was on a month-to-month lease. She was told that there were three spacious bedrooms, each with their own bathroom and tiny seating area on the top floor along with a shared living room and kitchen. The lower level contained a shared laundry room and a separate, locked storage area for each occupant.

The storage area was of little concern to her, since over the years she had reduced her belongings to that which would fit comfortably into a car. She had become a nomad of sorts, travelling from one part of the country to another for work. The only occasional tricky part was her mail so she kept a post office box in

Cincinnati, which she visited every couple of months when she met with her biggest client.

Andrea had received several, more lucrative offers over the years, but she truly enjoyed working with Cinci-Plastics. They were an honourable, family run company and although they were not that big of a company, they did good work and had good business ethics. In all of her contacts with the employees, she had been surprised at how happy and dedicated they all seemed. It was an unusual atmosphere to say the least. Her contact with employees for other clients was completely the opposite—everyone pointing fingers—no one doing anything productive to try to solve the problems. For that reason alone, she decided to work as often as she could for Cinci-Plastics and only when they had no work for her long term did she take on other assignments.

It wasn't that she needed the money. In addition to the fact that her clients paid all of her expenses, she also commandeered a hefty salary on top of that. She worked as much as possible, just to keep herself occupied. Since her clients paid all of her expenses, she had only a few bills to worry about and she paid those online. *Hope they have at least DSL out here but I doubt it,* she thought mindlessly as she lifted her luggage from the car.

She made her way to the front door and was about to knock when the door flung open, taking her by surprise.

"Hey y'all!" said the very attractive, tall redhead who opened the door.

"You must be our new roommate. We thought you might have got yourself lost," she added as she stepped aside to let Andrea make her way in with her luggage.

"I'm Justine," she said as she extended her hand.

"Andrea," she replied, taking the offered hand gently as she placed her duffle bag on the floor beside her. Just then, another woman appeared from what she presumed to be the kitchen.

"And that, would be Rebecca," Justine indicated with a nod over to the dark-haired woman making her way towards them.

"Hey," Rebecca said as she produced her hand for a welcome.

"I'm Andrea, nice to meet you," she replied, surprised at the firm handshake and appraising look she received from Rebecca.

"Why don't I show you to your room and let you get settled for a bit?" Justine suggested.

"Sounds good to me, it's been a long day," replied Andrea as she followed the tall redhead toward the door to their right.

"This is it," Justine exclaimed as she unlocked the door and handed Andrea the key.

The room was surprisingly spacious and inviting. There was a double bed along the wall just below the large window, which overlooked the vast wooded area that surrounded the house. The two large matching dressers would be more than adequate to hold the few articles of clothing Andrea owned. A twenty-inch flat-screen television hung from the wall opposite the bed above one of the dressers. The floors were a dark hard wood, which accented the colour of the log walls beautifully.

Off in the corner, sat a small seating area with two comfortable looking beige wrap-around chairs and a small round table. Next to that, was another door, which led to the private bathroom. A large fan hung from the high ceiling and added an additional touch of elegance to the already cosy décor.

Very nice, Andrea thought as she took in her living space for the first time.

"I'll leave you to get settled for a bit; then, when you're ready, I'll give you a tour," Justine suggested.

"Thanks," Andrea muttered as the beautiful woman left the room. She plopped herself down on the bed and looked around taking it all in. *This will suit me just fine.*

She took a minute to evaluate the two women she had just met. Both seemed friendly enough, but there was something about the dark-haired woman that she just wasn't sure of. It wasn't that she disliked her or anything; there was just something about her she couldn't put her finger on.

She made her way into the small, but comfortable bathroom and took a long hot shower before taking the time to unpack her belongings.

About an hour later, Andrea emerged from her room to find the other two women sitting on the couch watching television.

"Feel better?" Justine asked as Andrea approached.

"Much! Thanks."

"Come on, I'll show you around." Andrea followed as the redhead stood and made her way toward the kitchen.

"Wow!" she said as she entered the large eat-in kitchen that would make any chef envious. It was complete with top of the line stainless steel equipment and had enough pots and pans to prepare a meal for fifty people.

"Someone likes to cook!" Andrea said as she looked around the space, excited to be able to prepare an extravagant meal some day. She loved to cook, but hadn't been able to do much of it during the last few years because she'd been moving around so much and was rarely near a real kitchen.

"Not so much anymore," Justine replied somewhat solemnly.

Puzzled by the response, Andrea wanted to ask why, but thought it was too soon to start asking personal questions.

"Here's the fridge ... as you can see, we each have a shelf to keep things that are for our personal use. The rest of the fridge is for common things like ketchup and stuff that is shared among us. We all take turns buying those things." The spacious industrial refrigerator was more than adequate. Andrea took notice of the two shelves, which were labelled and full of food. One was labelled JB, which she assumed to be Justine's shelf. The other shelf was labelled H&R, so the R must be Rebecca, but who was the H?

Justine must have noticed the puzzled look on her face, because she quickly said, "This is my shelf." She pointed as expected to the one labelled JB. "This one belongs to Heather and Rebecca," she said as she pointed to the other shelf.

Just the sound of the name Heather sent Andrea's insides into a frenzy. Even after all these years, she still could not get the woman off her mind. She still carried so much regret over what had happened.

"Who's Heather?" Andrea asked in a voice so shaky she wasn't even sure it was her own.

"Heather actually owns the house. She and Rebecca have been dating for a while. Although Rebecca still has her own place, she mostly just stays here ... especially because Heather is rarely home with her job and all," Justine replied mater-of-factly as she began to lead them out of the kitchen.

Andrea quickly forced all memories of Heather from her mind, deciding instead to focus on the fact that Justine had mentioned that Rebecca was Heather's girlfriend.

Well, at least things are looking up. She didn't expect to run into many lesbians in this part of the country. *Wonder what the story is on Big Red,* she thought as she followed Justine from the kitchen to the staircase to her far left.

They made their way down the long stairwell to the lower level of the house. It was just as clean and well maintained as the rest of the house and contained a large laundry room and three separate caged storage areas. Andrea knew she would not need the extra space but took the key Justine handed her anyway.

On the way back up the stairs, Andrea asked Justine where she might find a grocery store since she hadn't seen anything on her way into town.

"I'll draw you a map," Justine said with a giggle. "Everything is concentrated in one area of town."

Andrea must have looked at her skeptically, because Justine convincingly added, "Really, we even have a Wal-Mart. Come on, I have some time if you want to take a ride out there right now."

"That would be great—are you sure you have time?"

"Yeah! Just let me ask Rebecca if she needs anything."

Five minutes later, Andrea was driving back down the long narrow driveway toward the gravel road, which led to the main road.

"Since you didn't see anything on your way in, I presume you came in from that way," Justine said as she pointed toward the East. "Turn right at the stop sign—it'll take you into town."

Andrea did as directed and was surprised to see that the farther she went, the closer the homes were together. Eventually, she found herself in the middle of the little town, surrounded by restaurants, shopping malls, and hoards of people.

"See, I told you," Justine said as she pointed to the Wal-Mart up the road. "It's one of those twenty-four hour superstores, which is handy, but if you're after groceries, the Food Lion right here is a bit cheaper."

Andrea decided that Justine didn't seem to want to go to Wal-Mart, so she made the left hand turn into the Food Lion parking lot instead. Making their way quickly through the grocery store aisles, Andrea realized just how hungry she was. She hadn't eaten all day, and she was putting things in her cart that she would not normally buy.

Never shop for groceries on an empty stomach, Andrea reminded herself as she took the cookies and potato chips out of her cart and replaced them on the shelves. She had always taken good care of herself, even as a teenager. She consciously avoided junk food and opted for fresh fruits and vegetables instead. Since she practically raised herself, one of her high school coaches was very influential in helping her understand the importance of good health and showed her how to eat properly and exercise.

After they finished shopping, Justine suggested they drive around town for a while so Andrea could become better acquainted with the area. Andrea tried to pay attention to everything Justine was pointing out, but she knew she would have to come back and explore on her own. There was just too much to take in all at once. The only thing she made sure to focus on, was the way home.

"Turn left at the Taco Bell," Justine said absent-mindedly as she took the time to return a text message on her cell phone. "Sorry about that ... my boyfriend is looking for me."

Well, that answers that question, Andrea thought with a grain of disappointment. They rode the rest of the way home in relative silence as Justine continued to text message her boyfriend in order to make plans to meet in a few hours. Andrea was surprised at how easily she found the little gravel road which led to the driveway without any influence from Justine.

Once home, she busied herself with unpacking her groceries and preparing an omelette for dinner. It was well after nine o'clock when she was through. Fatigue and anticipation about tomorrow were starting to set in, so she headed directly to bed after washing her dishes.

Although Andrea didn't have to be at the plant until Friday, she always found it best to get there a few days early and get to know the people she'd be working with on a daily basis. This would give her an edge when the problems started, and they most certainly would. The launch of a new vehicle was always difficult, and with so many parts and components coming from all over the world, there was bound to be something that didn't fit or didn't match. Spending a few days at the plant before the launch began was always helpful. If she could befriend some of the employees, they would be less likely to go ballistic if there were any problems with the parts her client was shipping them.

Andrea was also looking forward to seeing Carlos again. They had worked together on several occasions at various plants and had developed a good working relationship. When she heard that he was going to be the weekend launch supervisor, she felt a sense of relief. There was nothing worse than having a part problem on a weekend because no one wanted to be the one to call in the big bosses. They were at home enjoying time with their families, and didn't want to solve disputes with suppliers. Instead, they just overreacted and hassled the plants for replacements parts no matter who was at fault.

The cost of shutting down an assembly line was astronomical; and, the additional cost of sending replacement parts via airfreight was insane. Couple that with the added cost of overtime required to produce the replacement parts and it was enough to eat up any profit a small to medium size supplier would make for the year. That was why Andrea's job was so important. It was her job to diffuse any situation that arose, and often times, the assembly plants were a lot more lenient with suppliers who had good representatives present during launches.

Andrea had put her Sociology and Psychology degrees to good use over the years. She had great insight into what made people tick, and she knew how to get them to see things from her perspective. Her knowledge of people, along with her natural problem solving ability, and charming personality, helped her excel.

She hadn't sought out this career. It just fell into her lap after answering an ad for a job that required a lot of travel and good people skills. Once she had been at it for a while though, it was clear that this was what she was born to do. When word got around about how good she was at her job, the offers started coming in from all over, offering her astronomical amounts of money to help suppliers mend their relationships with the assembly plants. It wasn't until she was back at home, taking care of some outstanding legal issues, that she met with Cinci-Plastics for the first time. She knew from day one, that this was the client she wanted to work for, so one by one, she dropped the others and began working exclusively for Cinci-Plastics—a choice she'd never regretted.

Chapter 2

▼

Andrea woke to the sound of birds chirping and sunlight pouring into her bedroom. She'd have to remember to close the blinds if she ever wanted to sleep in, but today, the fact that she was up early was a good thing. Not only did she want to head to the plant early, she was extremely grateful that the night was over. The nightmares were worse than they had been in years, and more vivid than ever.

As she stood in the shower letting the water pour over her head, she tried to understand what had triggered the nightmares. Something must have happened yesterday that subconsciously brought back some old memories, but nothing in particular was coming to mind. After years of therapy, Andrea understood that she had to recognize the triggers in order to move past the memories on a subconscious level.

Determined to identify the cause, she got dressed and headed to the kitchen to have a bowl of cereal for breakfast before trying to replay the events of the day before. She was surprised to find Rebecca already dressed and in the kitchen reading the paper. Rebecca was wearing khaki shorts, a blue golf shirt, and a pair of work boots. She could not read the name on the shirt, but she assumed that whatever Rebecca did required her to work outdoors.

"Mornin'," Rebecca said, glancing Andrea's way momentarily, before returning her attention to the newspaper.

"Good morning," Andrea replied politely. She was glad that Rebecca didn't seem to want to chat. She needed to be alone so she could think.

When she opened the refrigerator to retrieve the milk for her cereal, it hit her like a ton of bricks. *It couldn't be that simple*, she muttered to herself as she looked at the H and R on the shelf below hers. *Could it be the name Heather that triggered the memories that caused the nightmares?* She poured the milk over her cereal and headed to the living room to eat so that she could be alone.

A single day hadn't passed over the last eight years that Andrea had not thought of Heather and wondered how she was and if she was happy, but those thoughts alone had never caused nightmares. Maybe it was the fact that she didn't allow herself to examine her feelings yesterday at the mention of the name Heather that caused a subconscious memory of her youth. She had learned over the years that it was best to allow the feelings to surface and deal with them as they came, rather than push them away, which is what she did yesterday. She stared off into space and allowed the memories to flood her mind.

Andrea climbed the trellis that led to Heather's second floor bedroom. It was dark, but she had made the climb almost daily during the previous ten years and could do it blind folded with both hands tied behind her back.

She quietly opened the window and shimmied through it, thankful for her slender build. Over the years, as her body developed, it was growing increasingly difficult to fit through the opening. At seventeen, she often felt a little childish sneaking into Heather's room at night, but she always felt like it was her special little secret, even though everyone knew she spent most nights there. Even Mrs. Johnson had told her, years before, that she was welcome to use the front door no matter what time it was.

Andrea rarely woke Heather if she was sleeping. She'd just crawl into bed next to her or sleep in the chair next to the bed. Tonight, though, she needed her best friend, so she sat at the edge of the bed and caressed Heather's face gently with a shaky hand until she opened her eyes.

"What's wrong?" Heather asked sleepily as she sat up.

"My mom's in the hospital ... she's unconscious," Andrea managed to say, before she started to sob uncontrollably against Heather's shoulder.

Rebecca, making her way from the kitchen to the front door, interrupted her thoughts.

"See you later," she said as the door closed behind her.

Andrea decided that further introspection at this point was useless since the anticipation of getting over to the assembly plant was starting to occupy her mind. She made a mental note to revisit the memory later on, when she had more time.

On the way to the plant, she stopped and picked up a couple dozen donuts. As small of a gesture as it was, the employees usually seemed appreciative.

After spending a few minutes charming the security guard, she was able to convince him to issue her a long-term guest pass as opposed to having to stop in every day and sign in as a visitor. This would save her a lot of time over the next several months. Especially if she was called in during the night or on a weekend when there was a different guard on duty.

Fifteen minutes later, she was standing in the reception area, donuts in hand, waiting for the receptionist to finish her phone call so that she could call down for an escort into the production area. When the perky brunette finally acknowledged her, she identified herself and requested an escort.

"Hi gorgeous. How was the flight from Jamaica?" Rebecca asked as Heather made her way through the front door.

"Nothing unusual—just the same old crabby people who are unhappy because their vacation is over," Heather replied with a sigh before she made her way to the couch to kiss Rebecca hello.

"I can't imagine being cooped up in a plane with all those people all the time."

"It's not so bad most of the time," Heather insisted.

"Hey ... I met our new roommate yesterday."

"What's she like?"

"She seems nice," Rebecca replied in a flat tone. "A little too athletic for my liking ... she's more your type."

"Sounds interesting," Heather replied seductively. "I'm going to take a shower and then you can tell me just how athletic she is," she added playfully before leaving the room.

Heather and Rebecca met about five years earlier at a party. Heather's girlfriend at the time, Donna, was a chef at the only fine dining establishment in town, and was a friend of Rebecca's. Over the years, Heather and Rebecca's friendship grew stronger, and two years ago, when Donna was diagnosed with breast cancer, it was Rebecca who helped Heather get through it. Although it was painful to watch Donna wasting away because of the terrible disease, it was almost more painful to watch Heather wasting away with her.

Before Donna got sick, Heather's fun and bubbly personality were what naturally drew people, including Rebecca, to her. As Donna's illness progressed, Heather's entire life became about caring for her, and Rebecca watched as the real Heather slowly dwindled away with Donna.

After Donna died, Heather was devastated. She took a leave of absence from her work as a flight attendant and locked herself away in her bedroom for weeks—refusing to see or talk to anyone. Although Rebecca understood the grief

Heather was feeling, she also knew that she needed to help Heather start to get her life back. Without consent, she simply began living in one of the spare bedrooms and forcing Heather to eat properly and to get out of bed to watch television once a day.

Within a month, Heather was able to get herself together, and even went back to work, thanks to Rebecca's constant pushing. Rebecca thought about moving back to her apartment, but Heather needed help maintaining the house and it just seemed more convenient, and less lonely to stay with her. So that's what she did, and things remained that way until about six months ago when they both had had too much to drink and ended up in bed together.

In the morning, when they had both sobered up and realized what they had done, they had a long talk. They decided, that since they were both single, consenting adults who seemed to enjoy each other's company, that Rebecca should move out of the spare bedroom and into Heather's.

Their quest for roommates began about three months ago out of necessity because Heather could no longer pay the bills on her own. Although Donna had life insurance, the hospital bills ate up the better part of it, and since Rebecca still kept her own apartment, she could not help with the bills either.

When Justine moved in, it was a godsend. Not only was she helping with the bills, her personality meshed perfectly with those of the other two. Heather was ecstatic at the news that a second roommate was now moving in and that her six-month lease had been paid in advance.

"The new roommate is athletic, you say," Heather said as she straddled Rebecca on the bed and teased her seductively, biting and kissing her neck.

"Yes, very," Rebecca replied.

"Is she gay?"

"Well, it's not like she was wearing a sign or anything, but I would say it's a safe assumption. There is something strangely familiar about her though."

"Does this gay, athletic, strangely familiar woman have a name?" Heather asked.

"I'm sure she does, but it escapes me right now," Rebecca answered before flipping Heather over and reversing their positions.

Spending a couple of hours at the plant was just what Andrea needed to get her world righted again after last night's nightmares. It took only a few minutes for her to get back into the swing of things as she made her way around the plant with Carlos.

She was overjoyed when Carlos greeted her in the reception area. He seemed equally happy to see her. They spent a few minutes talking about what each had been doing since they last worked together and then they decided a tour of the plant was in order.

Her mind automatically began to focus on her job, naturally anticipating what problems she would face later in the week when production began. In order to increase consumer buzz about the new car, there was a nation-wide contest to come up with the best name for the sporty two-seater. The winner of the contest would receive one of the new cars. The announcement as to the name of the car would be made on Saturday; allowing a couple of days for the nameplates to be made as the cars come off the assembly line. Until the car was named, it was known simply as Smith.

Although Andrea had seen many renderings of the car and several photos, they didn't do Smith justice. When Carlos brought her over to see one of the pre-production versions, she was shocked at its sleek lines and low profile. It wasn't typical of every other sports car on the market; it had a certain flair about it that made it special. It had personality and spunk with just the right mix of speed and aggression.

Carlos was called into an important meeting, so Andrea decided to mingle with some of the employees for a couple of minutes before quietly making her way back out to her car. She had the rest of the afternoon to herself, but before allowing herself to relax, she wanted to call Lorraine, who was the quality manager at Cinci-Plastics to make sure there were no surprises headed her way.

"Cinci-Plastics. How may I direct your call?"

"Hey, sexy! What are you wearing?" Andrea asked when she was certain it was Terri on the other end of the phone.

"Wouldn't you like to know?" Terri replied teasingly while looking around to make sure there wasn't anyone in earshot before continuing. "I miss you. When do you think you'll be able to come back for a visit?"

Andrea met Terri on her third visit to Cinci-Plastics. Terri had just started as the receptionist there, and Andrea was drawn instinctively to her bubbly personality and beautiful baby blue eyes. Although they weren't technically dating, anytime Andrea was in the area, they made a point of getting together.

"Probably not for a couple of weeks. I won't know until things get started here … you know how it goes."

"I can't wait. I know I just saw you a couple of days ago, but it was such a rushed visit I didn't get to enjoy your company as much as I would have liked to." Terri wasn't one to settle down with anyone, but out of all the women she dated, Andrea was definitely her favourite so she tried to be available anytime she was in town.

"I'm sorry I couldn't stay longer. I promise I'll make it up to you next time."

"I'll hold you to that promise. Now, who did you want to talk to besides me?"

"I only want to talk to you, but unfortunately I have to talk to Lorraine."

"Oh … sucks to be you!" Terri exclaimed with a chuckle.

"Great! I take it she's in a mood today?"

Andrea genuinely liked Lorraine but unfortunately, the company was at that awkward stage where there was too much work for the managers, but not enough work to justify hiring more staff. That meant that those who were working there were stretched to the limit. Since Lorraine's position was one of the most stressful and important positions, she was often in a foul mood.

"Oh Yeah! Good luck! Can't wait to see you. Bye!"

"Bye, Ter."

Andrea listened to the awful on-hold music for thirteen minutes before Lorraine finally picked up.

"Sorry Andrea, I was running some colour checks on some of your parts and wanted to get them finished before I talked to you," Lorraine said breathlessly.

"Any problems? And where is you lab tech? You shouldn't be worrying about doing colour checks."

"No. Broken leg. I know," Lorraine answered quickly, hoping to appease Andrea so she could get back to work.

"That sucks. I don't imagine you're going to be able to fly down here for the launch then?"

"I know they like to have everyone there, but I don't think I can leave with everything going on," Lorraine said.

"I'll take care of things at this end, but you make sure every part you send is a good one, and call me if you find anything that might even be the slightest bit off … no matter what time it is."

Andrea hated surprises. If there was going to be a part problem at the assembly plant she wanted to be the first to know about it so, if at all possible, she could take care of it before it became a crisis.

"Will do. Call me once things get going." This was Lorraine's way of politely dismissing Andrea and her sometimes-overbearing behaviour. Although Andrea's constant pestering had saved them a lot of trouble over the years, it was extremely irritating, especially when there were so many more important things Lorraine could be doing.

Andrea recognized the annoyance in Lorraine's voice and decided to take her cue and let her get back to work.

"Bye ..." Click. Lorraine had hung up the phone so quickly that Andrea didn't get to finish her sentence.

"Well, you have a nice day too!" Andrea added as she stared blankly at her cell phone.

With the rest of the afternoon to herself, Andrea decided that she would take a ride to the mountains to find a quiet place to be alone and put some more thought into what had caused her to start having nightmares again.

She wished she had brought the trail maps she had prepared before leaving Cincinnati, but unfortunately, she had left those, along with her hiking boots back at the house. Thankfully, the steel-toed boots she wore religiously to the assembly plants were well worn, and although heavy, were well treaded for hiking.

From her research, she remembered a small section of short trails in the river section of Pilot Mountain State Park. When she arrived, she thanked God and Terri for renting her an SUV. If she'd had a small car, she would never have managed to cross Horne Creek three times. Even as high as she sat off the ground, whenever she met up with a section of the creek, she stopped and carefully negotiated the crossing.

Stepping out of her car, she recalled that there were only a few miles of trails in this section, just enough to give her some peace and quiet to do some thinking. She made her way down the Bean Shoals Canal Trail towards the river, excited to be outside, enjoying the beautiful weather, instead of being cooped up in a hot, dusty plant.

When she reached the river, she looked to the left and the right. *Which way should I go?* She instinctively headed to the right and followed the easy trail along the river's edge. As she walked, she encountered several families and groups of fishermen huddled along the banks of the river. The rushing water appeared cold and almost threatening, but that didn't stop the thirty or so people who were either attempting the trek across the river, or simply swimming to cool off. Suddenly, she remembered the reason she was there. She was looking for solitude—somewhere to think.

Too many distractions, she decided. She turned around and began looking for another trail that would lead her away from the river. She headed down the first trail she found and once she was alone, she let her mind drift to a place she really didn't want to go.

Chapter 3

▼

The memory was as vivid as the day it happened.

Andrea had come home after soccer practice to get started on her chores and homework. As soon as she opened the front door, she knew something was wrong. The fact that her mother's car was still in the driveway was not all that uncommon. She routinely got a ride to work with one of her friends so that Andrea could use the car if she needed it. There was just an eerie feeling that overwhelmed her when she stepped through the threshold. Immediately, her stomach clenched and sweat began forming on her forehead. Although she had not seen her mother yet, she knew something was terribly wrong. She fought for each breath as her body's natural panic instincts took over. Each step was a conscious battle between mind and body.

Instinctively, she headed for the kitchen and that's where she first found her, laying limply on the floor with an almost peaceful look on her face. Had it not been for the pool of blood surrounding her and the fact that she was on the kitchen floor, she would have thought her mother was napping.

She opened her mouth to call out for her, but found she had no voice. Andrea approached slowly, afraid of what she might find. "God Mom, what did he do to you this time?" She had bruises all over her arms and legs. She tentatively reached for her mother's wrist to check for a pulse. She was both relieved and saddened to find a very faint pulse. Immediately, she rose to reach for the phone and dialed 911.

By the time the paramedics and police arrived, Andrea had found the spot on the corner of the kitchen counter where her mother had hit her head during the struggle. There were remnants of hair, flesh, and blood, and due to the position of her injury, it didn't take a forensic scientist to realize that she had not simply slipped during the struggle. Her head had been smashed against the corner of the counter top intentionally.

The memories caused an immediate wave of nausea to overtake her and she involuntarily lost the contents of her stomach. Andrea had experienced this before as part of her therapy, but it had been a long time since it had been this bad. Occasionally, she'd have a flashback or a dream, but they were usually minor, causing only an emotional reaction. Last night's nightmare was just as bad as the ones she'd had for the first year or so after the incident. She thought for a moment about calling her therapist, but there was no cell phone reception and she was confident the worst of the episode was over.

She continued down the trail and allowed herself to resume to memory, knowing it was the only way to move on.

Andrea wanted to ride in the ambulance with her mother but the police would not allow her to go to the hospital until she gave them a statement. They had never been called to the house before, so they were surprised to hear how often her father had acted violently toward her mother. She explained that her mother was extremely embarrassed by it and thought she could handle it on her own. Her mother had suffered some relatively serious injuries over the years, but since she worked at the hospital as a nurse, she was able to make up excuses about being clumsy, and get herself patched up without raising suspicion.

The police were reluctant to make her father the prime suspect automatically.

"Could have been a home invasion?" the one detective suggested to the other, who nodded his head in agreement.

"I'm telling you, HE did this," Andrea argued with them, trying to get them to understand.

"We understand miss, but we have to consider all possibilities," the younger detective said, trying to calm her down.

"Do you know where you father is right now?"

"No. May I go now?" Andrea replied coldly, wanting to go to the hospital to be with her mother.

"Sure, here is my card. Call me if you think of anything that may help us find out who did this," the older detective added nonchalantly.

"Miss, are you okay to drive?" asked the younger detective.

Andrea could tell he was being sincere, and she felt somewhat comforted by it.

"I'm fine ... I just want to get going," she insisted.

"We'll be in touch," the older detective said as he received confirmation from the forensic team that they had gathered all the evidence they needed and were ready to leave. On their way out, the younger detective turned, as if to say something to Andrea but simply looked at her in a knowing way, as if he knew what she was going through, and walked away.

Andrea had no time to think about the detective, she had to get over to the hospital. As she raced towards the hospital, alone for the first time in hours, the reality of the situation started to sink in. She knew her mother's injuries were serious this time. Her emotions were all over the map. She was scared and angry and she felt guilty for not going home right after school. Maybe she could have stopped him or at least distracted him long enough for her mother to escape. A small part of her almost wished her mother wouldn't survive this attack. Her mother had suffered so much over the years as a result of his violent behaviour, but she refused to leave him. She and Andrea had argued about her leaving him that very morning.

Andrea was so distracted, that she narrowly avoided hitting a car that had stopped to turn in front of her. The near miss was enough to allow her to focus on driving for the rest of her drive over to the hospital.

She didn't have to talk to the doctors to know that she would never speak to her mother again. When she walked into her room, the woman she saw was not her mother—she was a shell. She was hooked up to so many machines, it was clear that they were the only things keeping her alive. Her mother's head was swollen to twice its normal size, and her face was bruised, further evidence of the beating she'd suffered.

When the doctors did come in to speak with her, they only confirmed her initial assessment. They indicated that the machines were keeping her alive for the time being and that they had done all they could do for her for now. It would take several days to determine the extent of the brain damage.

Andrea, being her mother's only living relative, aside from the man who did this to her, would have some difficult choices to make over the next few days. She knew her mother wouldn't want to be kept alive by machines, but if there was a chance at a recovery, Andrea wanted to allow her that chance.

She spent several hours sitting by her mother's bed, holding her hand, trying to understand what makes a person do something like this, especially to someone, he supposedly loves.

It was just after midnight when Andrea went over to Heather's. She should have gone home to clean up the mess in the kitchen and to take a shower, but she was afraid. What if her father was home waiting for her? Heather was the only person who made her feel safe, and she was also the only person she had ever trusted enough to talk to about what her family life was like.

Andrea suddenly realized she had lost track of time. She looked around, trying to determine her location. The sun was beginning to set, and she realized that she had been walking for nearly four hours and that she had probably hiked nearly ten miles. She searched her memory for the map of the park, and although she didn't remember crossing a road, she knew was in the corridor between the river section and the mountain section of the park. She had no food and was nearly out of water, so she knew her only choice was to try to make it back to the car.

Thankfully, the trail was downhill the rest of the way and was clear enough to allow her to move rather quickly. She stopped for an hour as total darkness enveloped her. Although she wanted to keep going, with such poor visibility she could have easily tripped over something and sprained an ankle or worse. Finally, the moon began to crest over the top of the mountain and it provided plenty of light for her to make it the rest of the way to the car.

By the time Andrea reached the car, she was so in awe of her beautiful moonlit surroundings that she considered spending a little longer out there, but her grumbling stomach quickly reminded her that she had no food with her.

On the way home, she chastised herself for being so careless. It wasn't like her to be irresponsible like that. She never went hiking alone without at least a small pack of emergency supplies, even if it was just a short hike, like the one she'd planned on today.

It was well after eleven when Andrea pulled into the dark driveway. She had stopped at a sub shop on her way home to quiet the monster growing in her belly and was sufficiently full and exhausted by the time she arrived.

The house was in near darkness when she entered. Justine's room appeared quiet and dark, but she could make out the glimmer of candlelight emanating from the space beneath the door to Rebecca's room. She decided not to put any more thought into what might be going on behind that door since it would only lead to frustration. She hated being so far away from Terri, and Terri was right, her last visit had been short and had only served to rekindle the nearly dormant embers of her neglected libido. She quietly made her way to her room, took a long shower, and prayed for sleep to come quickly and easily.

By Saturday evening, Andrea was exhausted. She had put in two eighteen-hour days in a row and was happy to be home. The launch had gone extremely well. The winner of the contest was a young woman in New York who appropriately suggested the name Phoenix. The name suited the car perfectly. It was, after all, a creature raised from the dead. Production had stopped a few times for some minor tweaks, but overall, things were going well. So well in fact, that Carlos told her to take the next day off but to make sure she was close by if something came up. Never one to turn down a day off, she accepted his offer with thanks.

During the times when production stopped for a few minutes, Andrea took the time to mingle with the employees. One, in particular, had caught her attention on Friday. She was a petite woman with long blond hair pulled through a ball cap. She was too far away for Andrea to decipher the colour of her eyes, but she had a smile that could melt hearts. Whenever Andrea happened to glance her way, she noticed that the woman was watching her, but that she would quickly look away, afraid to meet Andrea's eyes.

She noticed that the woman spent most of her breaks and downtime with another woman who had long curly brown hair and a cocky personality. *Family,* she decided. Her assumptions about the woman were immediately confirmed when she noticed the small rainbow triangle tattoo on her forearm.

By Saturday, the two women had managed to work their way into a circle of people with whom Andrea was chatting. This time, when Andrea's eyes met hers, she didn't look away. The woman's piercing green eyes held Andrea's for just a little longer than necessary.

Cute, but so very young. Not that Andrea considered herself old at twenty-six. It was just that most of the time she had nothing in common with younger women. Probably because of her upbringing. She had been given so much responsibility, at such an early age, that she acted a lot older than she was. Her partying days, such as they were, had been over long ago.

Before Andrea knew it, the two women were standing directly in front of her. The blonde, suddenly shy again, was staring down at her feet and the brunette was doing the talking.

"Hi! I'm Jamie," she said with an outstretched hand, which Andrea immediately accepted.

"Andrea," she replied. "Nice to meet you."

"I'm Tammy," the blonde said softly, extending her hand almost awkwardly.

"Hi," Andrea replied with a smile, taking her hand gently, trying to reassure her.

Further conversation was brought to a halt by the sound of the horn indicating that production was about to resume. The two women quickly walked back to their assigned areas. Andrea definitely thought Tammy was cute, but she couldn't be more than twenty-two, which meant that they would have little in common. Perhaps at the least, she could make a couple of new friends.

On Andrea's way out that evening, Jamie had stopped her and told her that a group of them were heading to a club that night and invited her along. As much as a part of her wanted to accept Jamie's offer, she was simply worn out, so she politely declined and told her that she definitely would accept the next time. Andrea watched from a distance as Jamie relayed the information to Tammy. She looked genuinely disheartened by the news, but her expression quickly changed. Apparently, Jamie had told her that Andrea had agreed to go with them the next time.

Andrea had just stepped out of the shower and was getting dressed when her cell phone rang. Surprised that she was able to find it amongst her other belongings casually thrown on the bed in a heap, she answered it on the third ring.

"Reynolds," she said.

"Andrea, it's Carlos. I need you to come back ... your parts are off-colour." He was talking fast and Andrea was having a difficult time understanding him.

"Carlos, calm down. I just left an hour ago. What could possibly be wrong?"

"Your parts are off-colour," he repeated.

Andrea was sure he had to be mistaken. She had taken the time to examine most of the shipment that they were going to use over the rest of the weekend and didn't see any problems. She also knew better than to try to explain this to Carlos over the phone. He was excitable by nature, so when something went wrong at the plant he'd get really worked up.

"I'm on my way," she said reluctantly as she hung up the phone and finished getting dressed. *Dinner will have to wait.*

It was eight-thirty by the time Andrea returned to the plant and it took her about two seconds to spot Carlos standing in the center of a group of people with his hands flailing in the air, yelling things incoherently.

"I'm here. What's the problem?" she said as she reached the group and tried to gain his attention.

"Look," he said as he pointed to the door handle Cinci-Plastics had supplied. He was right. The part did appear to be a few shades lighter than the surrounding door panel. Carlos was clearly flustered. His hair was dishevelled. He had beads of sweat running down his face.

"Calm down, Carlos ... let's try to find out what happened ... okay?" She used a quiet reassuring tone, which seemed to be working. He took several deep breaths and followed Andrea on her quest to find the problem.

"Is this the box the parts came from?" she asked calmly.

When the woman on the line nodded yes, Andrea picked up the box and looked at the label. Then she checked the label to the part. They matched. *Okay, so it's not a mislabelling problem.* She looked at the rest of the parts on the door and then read the label again. She knew what had happened immediately when she read the colour description on the label. It read medium dark charcoal. It was very close in colour to ebony, and unfortunately, only a few part numbers off. Clearly, someone had taken the box of handles to the line without double-checking the part numbers. From a distance, you could easily mistake the two colours.

"Carlos, they're using the wrong parts. Check your master list." She stood silently as he cross-referenced the list to the part number on the box.

"Sorry," he said after he realized the mistake. He was clearly embarrassed, but Andrea liked him too much to gloat. Instead, she decided to help him get this problem fixed.

"How many went through like this?" she asked.

"Probably only a few. I stopped production as soon as they told me about it."

"Get these parts out of here and get the line going again. I'll help you replace the ones that have already gone through," Andrea offered.

"You don't have to do that. It was my fault. I shouldn't have called you in before checking into it."

"Carlos, let it go. I'm here already, and it will only take an hour or so. I might as well give you a hand."

"Thanks Andrea," he replied sheepishly as they began to work on replacing the door handles on the cars that had already moved down the line.

Chapter 4

▼

It was after ten o'clock when Andrea made her way through the front door. She was famished and immediately made her way to the kitchen to make a salad. She smiled and shook her head as she busied herself collecting the required ingredients. *If that man doesn't calm down, he's going to give himself a heart attack.*

She was happily chopping away at a green pepper when she heard the kitchen door swing open.

"Andie?" the familiar voice said.

Andrea didn't have to turn around to know to whom the voice belonged. Throughout her life, there were only two people who called her Andie, and one of them was dead. Her shaking hand stilled mid-air over the cutting board, and she took a deep breath before turning around.

"Heather," Andrea replied with a shaky voice.

It had been eight years since they'd had any contact. She couldn't believe that the woman she'd been trying to forget for all this time was standing with her in the kitchen. She watched as a range of emotions crossed Heather's face. For a brief moment, she was sure she saw a glimpse of joy, but it was quickly replaced by sadness, then rage.

Andrea's stomach churned with regret. She had caused the pain in Heather's eyes. They stood in silence for several minutes, neither woman trusting their voice. She had to say something, but her throat was dry, and what would she say. Andrea had no excuses. Nothing she said or did would make up for her actions.

Without warning, the kitchen door swung open again and Rebecca stepped through the door.

"Hey baby! What's taking you so long? I almost had to get started without you," Rebecca joked as she wrapped her arms around Heather's waist and planted a kiss on her cheek. *Oh my God! She looks just like Donna*, Rebecca thought as she looked from one woman then to the other.

"Come on, let's go!" Heather said, and took Rebecca's hand, nearly dragging her out of the room in her haste to get away from Andrea.

Andrea stood in the same spot for several minutes after the women left the kitchen, stunned at seeing Heather. Even more stunned at seeing Heather with Rebecca. Her appetite gone, she threw out the ingredients she had prepared and headed for her bedroom.

Rebecca tried in vain to get Heather's mind back on what they had started before she had left the bed to get a glass of water, but Heather was in her own little world. One, Rebecca really didn't want to visit again. She tried to be supportive.

"I hadn't realized it until tonight, when I saw the two of you together, but she really looks a lot like Donna. I'm sorry if that upsets you."

"Donna looked a lot like her," Heather said quietly, the realization almost too much to bear. Had she really chosen Donna as a substitute for Andie? Was losing Donna more painful because it was like losing Andie all over again?

"What?" Rebecca asked cautiously. It appeared to her that Heather wasn't thinking clearly. Maybe she just needed a good night sleep.

"Nothing … I'm tired … Can we just go to sleep." Heather felt the tears threatening. She no longer trusted her voice.

"Sure, baby," Rebecca said soothingly as she wrapped her arms around her and held her tight. "I'm sorry she upset you."

Heather fought back the tears until she knew Rebecca was sleeping; otherwise, she would have felt her sobbing in her arms and there was no way she could explain what was really bothering her. She thought it best just to let Rebecca believe that Andrea reminded her of Donna. It was easier that way, but there was nothing easy about any of this.

It had taken years to get over the anger, but the pain lived on despite her efforts to let it go. She'd thought about Andie every day. Occasionally she'd remember a fond memory, but more often than not, she relived that day eight years ago when Andie walked out of her life.

Andrea, lying in her own bed, staring at the ceiling, was reliving that day as well.

They were waiting at the airport. Heather was saddened by the fact that they were both headed to different colleges, several hundred miles apart, but they swore they'd keep in touch and visit often.

Andie had known all along that that wasn't the case. She had planned it very carefully. Each detail to be executed with extreme precision. She could not face the possibility of almost certain rejection, so she worked out a way that she'd never have to see Heather again. She had known for years that she was in love with Heather, but there was nothing she could do about it; Heather was straight. Andrea would not risk losing their friendship due to a declaration of love. She knew she shouldn't do it, but she needed a memory of Heather to keep with her forever. One simple kiss would have to do for the rest of her life.

Andrea had gone over the details time and time again. Her plane was leaving before Heather's, so just as they were getting ready to make the final boarding call for her flight, she directed Heather to a quiet spot behind a pillar, out of everyone's view, but close enough to the gate that she could disappear before Heather knew what was happening.

"Heather," Andrea said softly, before pulling her close. "Please forgive me for this."

Heather was confused, she had no idea what Andie was about to do. Andrea looked deeply into Heather's eyes, gently cupped her face, stepped forward, and kissed her softly, but thoroughly.

By the time Heather regained her composure and opened her eyes, Andie was gone, but she was elated. She had been waiting for Andie to kiss her for years, but she didn't expect it to happen like this. She watched as Andie's plane taxied down the runway and took off before heading to her gate to wait for her flight. She was so happy she could have made it to New York without the airplane, floating there on her own cloud.

She couldn't wait to talk Andrea that night. She'd finally get a chance to confess her true feelings. Feelings she had kept hidden at her mother's urging. "I think Andrea feels the same way, sweetheart, but she's been through so much. She needs to heal completely before she'll ever be able to love anybody again," her mother had told her. "Let her come to you ... your friendship is what's most important."

Heather knew her mother was right. Andie had been through more in a few short years than most go through in a lifetime. For years, she followed her mother's advice, waiting for Andie to make the first move. There had been a few times where she was certain Andie was going to kiss her, but then she didn't. She thought that maybe her mother was wrong, and that Andie did not share her feelings, so she continued to keep her own feelings hidden. A difficult task, especially when they spent so much time together and even shared a bed on most nights.

The kiss was wonderful. She had dreamt of what Andie's lips would feel like. Soft, wet, warm. They were that, and so much more. It was as if a surge of electricity had passed between them. It was so powerful, she felt it in her toes.

As soon as her flight landed, she checked her cell phone. Andie had not called. Maybe she was scared. Maybe she was waiting for Heather to call her to tell her it was okay. More than okay, she thought as she dialed Andie's number.

"We're sorry, the number you have dialed is no longer in service, please check the number, and try your call again," the automated voice said.

She checked the number, and even though it was correct, she tried again, hoping for a glitch in the system or something. When she heard the same automated voice answer again, she started to worry.

After settling into her dorm room, she sat anxiously by the phone, waiting for Andrea to call. Maybe she lost her cell phone. Maybe she was busy getting settled. Maybe she didn't enjoy the kiss as much as Heather had. That last thought was too upsetting to consider any further.

As the weeks went on, Heather's concern turned into resentment and anger. Who was Andie to make the decision to end their relationship? After a few months, Heather accepted the fact that Andie was never coming back, and she began the painful process of trying to move on.

Andrea tossed and turned in her bed. There was no possible way she could sleep knowing that the love of her life was sleeping in the room next to hers with another woman. She knew there was only one solution. First thing in the morning, she would tell Heather she was moving out. She'd go get a room at a hotel near the plant. Hopefully, that would be enough distance to allow her to recover from seeing Heather again. *How did this happen?* She was never supposed to see her again, especially not looking as sweet and sexy as she did in her cotton boxers and tank top. She had grown into a beautiful woman. Even more reason to find somewhere else to live. Despite the memories, she would only be torturing herself if she stayed.

Heather never did fall asleep. She spent the night reliving the day of the kiss. *If only she wasn't so drop dead gorgeous.* She hadn't changed all that much, Heather noted. Her strong, sexy, androgynous facial features were even more prominent now. Her short dark hair was a shade lighter than she remembered, but her body looked just as fit as it did in high school when she played all those sports. Her steel-grey eyes were as intense as ever, revealing nothing. It just wasn't fair that she could reappear in her life after eight years and stir all the emotions she had fought so hard to bury. One minute she was having a great time with Rebecca, the next minute, her world had been turned completely upside down.

The instant the sun began to peek through her bedroom window, Andrea began to pack up her belongings. Once again, she was thankful that she didn't have many possessions—just a few bags of clothes and her laptop. She was exhausted and even more grateful to have the day off. After she checked into the hotel, she'd be able to get caught up on her sleep. *Hopefully*. She took a shower, hoping it would make her feel human again, but it wasn't much help.

She placed her bags near the door and made a pot of coffee while she waited for Heather to get up. Andrea had consumed nearly half the pot while watching the early morning news before Heather joined her in the living room.

"Look, Heather. I had no idea this was your house, I'll be gone in a few hours," Andrea said quickly before she completely lost the ability to speak.

"Don't leave on my account," Heather replied after a few seconds of uncomfortable silence. For a moment, Andrea thought Heather might forgive her, but when she continued, she realized that was not the case.

"We're two grown adults … we should be able to live under the same roof without it being a problem; besides, we're not likely to see that much of each other," Heather reasoned.

Okay, she's still angry, Andrea thought.

"It's your house Heather … I don't want you to be uncomfortable with me here."

"I'm not the one who should be uncomfortable," Heather replied accusingly.

Ouch! I guess I deserved that. Andrea braced herself for more, but Heather stormed off into the kitchen without another word.

Andrea believed in fate. Everything happened for a reason. Ending up in Heather's house after all this time was no coincidence. There had to be a reason she was there. She couldn't really leave now anyhow. Heather had practically dared her to stay. Leaving would only prove Heather right.

The unusually cool summer night sent shivers through Andrea's body, but the chill outside was nothing compared to the chill in the house where Heather was.

Maybe this isn't such a good idea she thought for the umpteenth time. Staying was more difficult than she could ever have imagined. Her body trembled at memory of the icy blue glare she received when she had walked into the living room an hour earlier and found Heather cuddled up on the couch reading a book.

Andrea had finally fallen asleep thanks to the help of a little pink pill and woke with the telltale dry mouth and grogginess. She hadn't left her room since she'd retreated to it after her encounter with Heather that morning, but now, she had no choice.

She needed something to drink and since it was after nine o'clock at night, she also needed to eat—something she hadn't done in over twenty-four hours.

A shaky hand held the doorknob for several seconds before it found the courage to turn it. She did not want to run into Heather again. Unfortunately, Heather was on the couch and there was no way to avoid her on the way to the kitchen.

She met Heather's eyes for a fraction of a second—they were like daggers, piercing the very depth of her soul. Andrea quickly averted her eyes and made her way to the kitchen. She reached for a bottle of water and a granola bar and descended the staircase adjacent to the kitchen that led to the outdoor patio below.

Andrea hadn't realized her hands were shaking until she fought with the packaging of the granola bar, unable to steady them enough to open it. Frustrated with her attempt, and her inability to control her emotions, she placed it on the table and opted for the water first, hoping it would calm her nerves enough to allow her to resume normal function of her body.

She sat for close to an hour, finally managing to open the granola bar. She was cold and tired but still not ready to face Heather again. Andrea felt, more than saw, the shadow appear from the room above her. She knew it was Heather but did not turn around to look up.

Why am I doing this to myself? Heather asked softly, as she pressed her hand against the windowpane. It was surprisingly cool.

I should have let her go ... but I didn't ... I practically asked her to stay.

A war was raging within her as she stared down at the woman she both loved and loathed. The two powerful and conflicting emotions were causing her inner turmoil. She was restless, uneasy, and unfocussed. She had to distance herself for a few days until she regained control of her emotions. Knowing she wasn't scheduled to work for a couple of days, she called her friend Laurie at the airport and asked if there was a jump seat available on a flight to anywhere but here.

She packed a bag and called Rebecca, who was staying at her apartment for the night, and told her she was called into work and would be back on Friday. Rebecca agreed, thinking that Heather was upset about Donna. She did not know how to console her. Maybe it would be best if she got away for a few days.

Heather was happy that Rebecca didn't put up a fuss the way she usually did when she was called into work unexpectedly. She sounded almost pleased about it. There was no way she was going to discuss her problem with Rebecca; so, if she didn't have to see her, she wouldn't have to talk about it. *Just let her keep believing it's about Donna.*

Andrea watched Heather's car pull out of the driveway. Relieved, she made her way back upstairs to her room and took a long hot bath to try to shake the chill from her body.

Chapter 5

▼

Five days had passed, and Andrea was starting to feel like herself again. Heather had not returned to the house since she'd left on Sunday night. Things were going well at the plant, but she'd been spending a lot of extra time there just trying to stay busy—to keep her mind from drifting to Heather.

She was sitting comfortably on the couch, watching television when Rebecca sat down to join her.

"Hey, how's it going?" Andrea asked tentatively. Rebecca rarely spoke to her, and she wasn't sure if Heather had filled her in on the details of their past.

"Been better," Rebecca responded. "It's been a long week."

"No kidding!" Andrea agreed with a smile, still unsure of Rebecca's motives.

"Are you going to be home tomorrow night?" Rebecca asked.

"I'll probably be home," Andrea replied evenly.

"Good, because I'm throwing a surprise birthday party for Heather tomorrow night, and since I planned it kind of last minute, there aren't a lot of people available," Rebecca said with a frustrated sigh.

Andrea tried to look surprised at the news of Heather's birthday, but it was a day she would never forget. For the last eight years, she'd celebrated Heather's birthday by buying a cupcake and blowing out a candle with a wish for Heather to be happy wherever she was.

"She seems so down this week ... I just want to do something to cheer her up," Rebecca added.

I'm certainly not the one to help with that, Andrea thought, as she tried to come up with a sound excuse to get out of attending Heather's birthday party. When nothing plausible came to mind she simply replied, "I'm sure a party will do the trick." *Not likely if I'm there. Maybe I'll make an excuse about being called into work.*

"I hope so," Rebecca added as she rose from the couch and left the room.

Terrific! How do I end up in these situations? Now, what do I buy her for her birthday?

If the Gucci she was sporting on her wrist the other night was any indication, Heather still had an unusual appreciation for fine timepieces. Andrea never understood Heather's watch fetish. She knew women who had a thing for shoes or handbags, but Heather was the only one she knew who loved nice watches. It was something that started when she was about fourteen, and every time there was an occasion for gift giving, Heather had always wished for a new watch.

Over the years, Andrea had saved what little money she could to make sure she bought Heather the best watch she could afford. Most of the time, they were cheap knock-offs, but now, she could afford to buy anything she wanted. The question was, would Heather reject the gift as a bad attempt to buy her forgiveness, or would she accept it for what it was—a generous gift that she would have given her years ago had she been able to?

After spending several hours researching jewellers, store locations, and watches online, Andrea decided that she'd head over to Hanes Mall in the morning after checking in at the plant for a few hours. There was no point sitting around the house all day if Heather was going to be home.

Andrea's trip to the plant was uneventful. Everything was going smoothly and even Carlos seemed more relaxed today than she had ever seen him. She had spent a few minutes chatting with Jamie and Tammy who reminded her that she promised to go out with them this weekend. Unsure of how long she'd have to stay at the party to satisfy Rebecca, Andrea told the young women that she would meet them at the bar around midnight. Jamie wrote out the directions for her on a piece of paper that conveniently had Tammy's cell phone number on it. *Not too subtle are we?*

Although Tammy still seemed nervous and somewhat shy, she was starting to open up a bit. Throughout the week, she and Andrea had talked about many different things, and Andrea was surprised to find Tammy to be very intelligent. She was also impressed by the fact that Tammy seemed to have her life together, despite her young age.

The traffic near the mall on a Saturday morning was awful. It took nearly twenty minutes to travel three blocks. She didn't even bother to look for a parking space near the door, opting instead, for the first one she saw at the far end of the lot. From her research the night before, she knew that there were two jewellers in the mall that carried Movado watches. They were conveniently located across from each other. If the first one didn't have what she was looking for, there was a good chance the other one might.

Mind made up and focussed, she put her no nonsense face on, and marched through the mall like the woman on a mission that she was. Helzberg's was her first stop and luckily, they had the Movado Amarosa she had chosen. With a thousand dollar price tag, there were certainly less expensive watches available, but this wasn't about the price. The beautiful, two-toned, stainless steel timepiece had a striking black face and diamond accents. It was simple but elegant—sleek and powerful—yet subtle and delicate. It personified everything that Heather was.

Andrea asked the young sales clerk to gift-wrap it, and set out on a mission that would prove to be even more difficult than choosing a gift—finding the perfect card.

After reading nearly every birthday card in sight, Andrea gave up, and opted for a blank card with a picture of an adorable puppy sporting a birthday hat. She would have to come up with the right words to say without upsetting Heather any more. It couldn't be too mushy, and a funny card wouldn't be well received.

How had Andrea's wonderfully simple life become so complicated all of a sudden? The last few years had been the most amazingly carefree of her life. She had lovers when she wanted them—she had tranquility when she wanted it—she answered to no one, and enjoyed every second of her solitary lifestyle. Suddenly, she was forced to deal with a decision she made eight years ago. Up until recently, she had convinced herself that it had been the right decision. She had gotten over most of the pain, and had moved on with her life; now, she was second-guessing herself. She had no idea that Heather was a lesbian. She had no idea if Heather knew it back then or if it was something she had recently discovered.

The fact that she threw away the most amazing friendship she had ever known because of fears that Heather would reject her if she knew the depth of her feelings was a difficult thing to get over—but for the most part, she had done so. The realization that Heather may have shared her feelings at the time, and that she threw it all away for nothing, was tearing her up inside. She had to find a way to break through the barriers and at least get Heather to talk to her. She knew forgiveness was too much to ask for, but they once shared a bond so tight that there still had to be something left there to build on.

Card in hand; she stopped back off at the jewellers to pick up the watch, which had been gift-wrapped exquisitely in fine gold leaf paper with a matching bow. A quick glance at her watch told her she had just enough time to run home and jump in the shower before the guests started to arrive.

Shortly after seven o'clock, the first group of guests began to arrive. Rebecca had taken Heather out for dinner to celebrate and they were scheduled to return at around eight-thirty. Justine had purchased the cake, and she was helping her boyfriend prepare a few appetizers in the kitchen while Andrea chatted casually with Julie and Connie, a couple of Heather's co-workers.

"So you are the new roommate," Julie said inquisitively as she looked Andrea over from head to toe.

Andrea was starting to get the uncomfortable feeling that everyone was watching her and it was more than just idle curiosity. There was definitely something going on here that she was oblivious to.

"Yeah, I moved in almost two weeks ago."

Julie looked from Andrea to Connie and said, "I can't believe how much she looks like Donna."

"No wonder Heather's been so freaked out lately," Connie replied.

Andrea was growing even more uncomfortable. She had to know what was going on.

"Who is Donna?" Andrea asked innocently.

Julie looked up at her almost as if she had been slapped across the face. "You mean they didn't tell you?"

"Tell me what?"

"Wait here," Julie said as she stepped toward the front door to retrieve something from her purse. "This is Donna," she said, holding up a picture of Heather and Donna.

"Holy shit!" Andrea exclaimed. No wonder all of Heather's friends were staring at her oddly. She did look exactly like Donna; in fact, if she didn't know any better she would have guessed it was a picture of herself with Heather.

"No kidding … Rebecca said you looked a lot like Donna, but until we actually saw you," she took a deep breath and paused, looking over at Connie for a moment before continuing, "Well, it's almost like seeing a ghost."

Andrea stood there dumbfounded for several seconds. Not only did she look exactly like one of Heather's previous lovers, the woman had apparently died.

"Donna's um …"

"Dead … yes," Julie interrupted. "She died of cancer about two years ago. Heather took it really hard."

"Okay people, we've got five minutes," Justine yelled over the crowd, putting an end to their conversation. "Y'all know what to do."

Obediently, everyone made their way silently to the kitchen and turned the lights out. They had all parked their cars safely out of sight in an open field behind the house. Andrea's heart rate began to quicken in anticipation of the big moment when Heather would walk through the door and they would all yell surprise. She tried to focus on the moment, but she was having a hard time clearing her mind of the information she had just learned. Why hadn't anyone told her? Maybe Rebecca's apparent dislike of her stemmed from the fact that she looked like Donna. Maybe it would have been best if she had just left that morning as she had planned. It was bad enough subjecting Heather to seeing her after what she had done, but to top it off, she looked just like her dead girlfriend. Andrea couldn't imagine what her presence in this house was doing to Heather.

"They're here!" Justine whispered, causing everyone in the room to still. Twenty seconds later, they heard the front door open and footsteps heading their way.

When the kitchen door finally opened, everyone yelled, "Surprise!" catching Heather completely unaware. Very rarely did a surprise party go off without a hitch. Usually someone slipped up and mentioned it, or the guest of honour suspected it. Not this time though. Heather was definitely surprised. In shock almost. She began making her way around the room greeting everyone with warm hugs and smiles.

Andrea was suddenly trying to find a way to escape the kitchen so that she would not have to put Heather through the awkward scene of hugging her. There was no subtle way out of the kitchen from where she was standing in the far corner of the room.

Everyone would notice her leaving. Unfortunately, everyone would also notice if Heather didn't greet her the way she had everyone else.

As Heather approached, their eyes met briefly, and the happiness that filled those eyes when she first entered the room, was quickly replaced with sadness. Andrea longed to make that sadness go away.

"Happy Birthday, Heather," Andrea whispered into her ear as she embraced her uncomfortably. Heather felt rigid in Andrea's arms, as if it was painful to hug her. It probably was, emotionally at least.

Heather was not prepared for the reaction her body was having to being in Andie's arms again. She didn't want to let go. Not now. Not ever. Despite her brain reminding her how much she detested this woman, her body was acting of it own accord, almost screaming to get closer—to hold on tighter.

This is insane, Heather thought and abruptly stepped out of Andrea's embrace and walked over to Rebecca without looking back.

Despite herself, Andrea found that being in close proximity to Heather was exciting her. There was definitely chemistry between them and no matter how angry Heather was; Andrea knew she had felt it too. Her body tingled everywhere Heather's had made contact with hers.

All these years, Andrea thought that it was she who'd made the ultimate sacrifice. She knew Heather would be hurt by her actions, but she thought that after a while, Heather would forget all about her, and that she would be the one left alone to suffer in silence. Never once, did she stop to consider that Heather might have felt the same way about her. No wonder she was so angry. How was she ever going to get Heather to forgive her?

Andrea watched as the guests mingled and chatted like one big happy family. It was clear that Heather had many close friends. She wasn't surprised. Growing up, Andrea was mostly a loner, but Heather seemed to be friendly with everyone. More often than not, when Heather's other friends invited her to go out with them, she'd decline their invitations and spend her free time with Andrea. She should have known then. *How could I have been so blind?*

For the first time since she'd found out about Heather and Rebecca's relationship, Andrea allowed herself to observe them from a distance. They seemed happy enough. Laughing, talking, joking, touching. *Touching.* Although she had no right to feel the way she did, she could not help but feel the fury building whenever Rebecca touched Heather.

Their eyes met across the room when Rebecca lifted Heather off the ground in an embrace. She was certain for a moment that Heather looked almost apologetic, but Andrea didn't care. She couldn't stand it any longer. It was just too painful to watch Heather in someone else's arms.

"Put me down," Heather insisted, trying to get out of Rebecca's bear hug.

Although Andrea's eyes never showed emotion, Heather knew all of the little quirks that gave away what she was feeling. When Andrea was nervous, she'd fidget with her bracelet. When she was happy, she hummed. When she was angry, she would clench and unclench her fists. When she was sad, like she was right now, she would look off into the distance trying to find that happy place. She was not ready to forgive Andie, she wasn't sure she ever would be, but she also wasn't so cruel that she wanted to subject her to watching Rebecca manhandle her either.

The least she could do was explain to Andie that her relationship with Rebecca meant nothing, that they were just passing time. But why should she? Andie had given up the right to concern herself with who Heather was seeing a long time ago when she walked out of her life. Somehow, seeing her so sad made Heather's anger melt just a little bit. She had to tell her, and she had to do it now.

"I'll be right back okay?" she said to Rebecca when she lowered her back down to the ground. Rebecca nodded and headed to the kitchen to retrieve another beer before rejoining the group they had been chatting with.

Heather looked everywhere for Andie. She didn't see her go into her room so she checked the patio downstairs. It was there that she noticed the taillights of a car heading down the driveway. She was too late. Andie was already gone. As she turned to walk back toward the stairs, she noticed something on the table. It was a small package with her name on it.

She opened the card and smiled at the cute little puppy that greeted her. After she opened it, she knew why it had been left out there instead of upstairs with the others. If Heather had opened this in front of the group, they definitely would have noticed her reaction. A single tear formed as she read the card.

Heather,
They say time is supposed to heal all wounds. The question is, how much time? I understand that eight years hasn't been enough time, but what you need to know is that I'm prepared to wait an eternity. I know I hurt you, and there is no excuse for that, so I won't blame you if you never find it in your heart to forgive me. Just know that I love you, and not a day has passed that I didn't think of you. I hope you like your gift. I wish I had been able to get you something this nice when we were kids. Happy Birthday, Heather.
Always,
Andie

With shaky hands, she opened the small box, already sensing what was inside, but not wanting to believe it. She wanted so badly to stay angry with Andrea. It was easier that way. No matter what her body wanted, her heart was still broken. She carefully removed the watch from its case and placed it on her wrist. *Oh, Andie ... I can't believe you remembered.* It was beautiful. It looked perfect on her wrist, almost as if it was made just for her, even though she knew it wasn't. She'd had her eye on this very watch, but could never afford to buy it.

Chapter 6

▼

As she reached the end of the long driveway, Andrea stopped the car and allowed herself to cry. She had no idea what she was going to do about her current situation. She knew she wasn't strong enough to sit back and watch Rebecca and Heather together. Maybe she should just move out. It may hurt at first, to walk away, but she would recover again, just as she did the first time. Or did she really ever get over Heather at all? Maybe that's why she never settled down? Maybe she enjoyed this job so much because she got to move around and never got tied down to anyone or anything. Sure, she had Terri, but that was more of an arrangement than a relationship. Had she been afraid to give her heart to anyone, or was it because it still belonged to Heather?

It wasn't even ten o'clock and she knew the bar would be empty this early, but she decided to head over there anyhow. Maybe she'd meet someone tonight to take her mind off Heather.

As she suspected, the parking lot was nearly empty. Being a private club, she knew she'd have to fill out a member application, and did so quickly, without incident, and paid the twenty-five dollar membership fee.

The place looked just like she'd envisioned it. It was a typical dance club. A huge dance floor with a few tables and booths scattered around its perimeter. Despite the fact that there were only six or seven people in the club at that hour, the music was already blaring, pulsating through her body. There were two men on the dance floor clearly enjoying the effects of ecstasy as they gyrated to the music completely uninhibited.

Andrea was usually very mindful of the fact that her father was an alcoholic and was very careful to avoid more than just the occasional drink from time to time. Tonight, though, she didn't care. She wanted it all to go away. She wanted to forget. Forget the past and the present.

"Captain and Coke ... Keep 'em coming," she said as she took a seat at the bar and handed the young man a one-hundred dollar bill.

Heather hadn't slept much. She waited up listening for Andie to come home—her concern growing by the hour. Here it was, eight in the morning, and Andie hadn't been home or even called. She knew she couldn't share her concern with anyone. They would ask why and she couldn't tell them ... especially Rebecca.

The sensation felt odd. It was as if someone was rubbing sandpaper on her cheek. Andrea willed it to be a dream but when it wouldn't stop, she forced one eye open. The sunlight emanating through window was blinding and she closed her eye immediately. She heard the telltale purring of a cat and slowly opened her eyes to gather her senses. She didn't know anyone with a cat; nevertheless, here it was, sitting on her pillow, licking her cheek. She looked around the room slowly, trying to ignore the spinning in her head. She had no recollection of the night before. The last thing she remembered was seeing Tammy and Jamie walk into the club ... After that, it was all a blank.

The room was tastefully decorated with high-end furniture, but nothing seemed familiar. Andrea struggled to sit up, but the nausea grew with every movement, so she lay back down and tried not to move.

"Hey, sleepy head!" Tammy said softly, as she entered the room with a tray of food.

Andrea looked at her and panicked. "Did I ... Did you ... Did we? Oh God!"

Tammy smiled gently as she sat next to Andrea on the bed.

"Nothing happened. I tried, but by the time I brushed my teeth and joined you in bed, you had already passed out," Tammy said in an amused tone.

"Thank God!" Andrea replied.

She noticed the sad expression on Tammy's face and added, "I didn't mean it like that ... It's just that, I would like to think I'd remember it."

Tammy seemed to understand. Her expression became soft and friendly again.

"Get down, Mr. Snickers," she said as she gently shooed the cat off the bed and urged Andrea to sit up.

Despite the nausea and the spinning in her head, Andrea complied and they sat facing each other, legs crossed in front of them, on the bed. The tray of food was resting between them.

"This isn't how I envisioned sharing breakfast in bed with you," Tammy teased. "Here, eat the bacon, it will help," she told Andrea.

Andrea gingerly nibbled at the crispy bacon, surprised at how easily it went down. She reached for a second piece, starting to feel a little bit better already.

"I'm sorry. I don't usually drink. Thank you for … everything."

"There's no need to thank me. It was selfishness on my part more than anything. Jamie was going to take you to her place, but I thought that maybe you and I might …" She blushed and looked away.

"I'm so sorry," Andrea said softly as she reached for Tammy's hand and took it in hers. When Tammy still wouldn't look at her, she reached across and lifted her chin with her other hand so their eyes met.

"It's okay."

"I guess I should have asked this last night, but um … are you seeing anyone?" Tammy asked.

Andrea smiled. She genuinely liked this woman and that's why she knew they would never be together. Tammy deserved more than what Andrea would ever be able to offer her and that is why, despite Tammy's willingness, Andrea would never cross that line.

"I don't usually get attached," Andrea replied.

Suddenly ashamed at the way that sounded, she continued, "I mean, with my job, I move around a lot—sometimes for months at a time. It tends to complicate the whole relationship thing."

"Don't you ever get lonely?"

"Sure, but I have a lot of friends all over the country. So wherever I am, there's always a friend nearby."

Tammy didn't believe her. "Do you want to talk about it?"

"About what?" Andrea didn't talk about personal things with anyone, she never did; except with Heather, or her psychologist.

"About what's bothering you? No one drinks as much as you did last night, unless they're trying to forget something, or have a drinking problem and you don't strike me as an alcoholic. I mean, I see you everyday at work and you clearly haven't been out drinking," Tammy noted.

"How'd you get to be so smart?" Andrea asked, trying to delay answering the question as long as possible.

"Years of being on my own I guess." She paused but knew she had to explain. "My parents and my little brother were all killed in a car accident when I was fifteen," Tammy explained.

Andrea interrupted her with some insight of her own, "And you feel guilty that you survived."

"How'd *you* get to be so smart?"

"My father was an alcoholic. He was abusive. He killed my mom," Andrea replied evenly.

"And you feel guilty that you couldn't stop him," Tammy interrupted.

Both women sat in awe staring at each other. Although it happened under different circumstances, they both shared a common fate. They had lost their families to tragedy, and had been powerless to prevent it from happening. They were left to deal with the pain and the memories.

Andrea was getting uncomfortable. She never talked to people about her past. As far as she was concerned, her life started when she took the job at Cinci-Plastics. Everything that happened prior to that had brought her nothing but grief and sorrow. Even Terri knew only the slightest details of her past despite being Andrea's lover and closest friend.

"I should get going," Andrea said as she stood to get out of bed.

"You don't talk about it much, do you?"

"Never," Andrea replied coldly. "Could you call me a cab so I can pick up my car?"

Tammy knew Andrea needed to talk about the things that were bothering her, but she didn't want to push. They hardly knew each other, and Andrea was hung-over, and clearly in no mood to talk.

"Your car is in the driveway. Keys are by the door, as are your shoes." She watched as Andrea slipped her jeans over her tanned, perfectly toned legs.

"You can't run away from your problems ... You can't drink them away either."

"I know, I just need some time," Andrea replied.

Tammy was easy to talk to and she understood more about Andrea's grief than most people ever would. Unfortunately, it was her mistakes with Heather that were consuming her now, and it wouldn't be fair to subject Tammy to that.

"Let me take you to dinner later this week when I'm feeling human again. We'll talk. It's the least I could do."

"The very least," Tammy replied with a hint of a smile.

"In case no one's ever told you this before ... you're one amazing kisser," Tammy added shyly.

Andrea blushed. She had been told that before, but usually it was in the heat of passion and she never put much thought into the compliment.

"Thanks, I guess. But I don't think ..."

"Yeah, I know. It's not going to happen. I understand. I'd like to think we could be friends though."

"I'd like that," Andrea admitted freely. Somehow, she had to ease out of this situation gracefully. She didn't want to hurt Tammy's feelings; not only because they had to see each other at work, but because she genuinely liked her, and they seemed to have a special connection.

"So dinner this week, then?" she asked with raised eyebrows, awaiting a response.

"On one condition?" The statement was more of a question and she met Andrea's eyes with a serious look on her face. Andrea nodded for her to continue.

"No more drinking."

Andrea was caught off guard by the pleading look on Tammy's face. She couldn't have denied her request if she'd wanted to.

"Deal."

When Tammy continued to look at her skeptically, Andrea added, "I promise."

Heather's concern for Andrea turned into anger when she walked through the front door just before one o'clock, looking like she'd been up all night partying. Her clothes, the same one's she'd had on the night before, were wrinkled. The stale stench of alcohol and cigarette smoke wafted into the room ahead of her.

"You look like hell," Heather said bitterly.

"Thank you," Andrea responded sarcastically and went directly to her room. She was not in the mood to argue with Heather today. It was none of her business anyhow. She had Rebecca to worry about.

A long shower helped to wash some of the grungy feeling from her body but she still felt awful—physically and emotionally. What she had done last night was foolish and she knew it. What if Tammy hadn't shown up? Who would she have gone home with? Worse yet, what if she had tried to drive home?

Never again, she said to her reflection in the mirror. It was a dangerous, self-destructive path she was headed down, and she knew the warning signs. She knew what alcohol did to her family, and from the look in Tammy's eyes this morning, she knew that alcohol had played some part in the loss of her family as well.

She had to get over this or it would eat her alive. It was all of her own doing. She had caused this. If she couldn't get over it, she would have to leave. She had no choice.

The sheets felt cool and crisp against her bare skin as she crawled into her own bed and closed her eyes searching her mind for happy memories settling on one that she often used when she was sad.

It was the first time she almost kissed Heather. It had been three months since her mother's death and Heather had finally convinced her to go out and have some fun. It was the annual Fourth of July county fair. Andrea hadn't left the house except out of necessity since the day her mother died. She had become a recluse of sorts, and although she'd let Heather visit, she hardly spoke to her. Heather would tell her about all the local gossip and make sure she'd eaten, but mostly they just sat in silence. It was Andrea's way of grieving, but it was also her way of putting some distance between herself and Heather. Her attraction toward Heather had grown exponentially after her mother's death since she had no one else to focus on.

Prior to that day, she had always refused Heather's invitations to go out to parties or to see a movie. Andrea couldn't bear the pitiful expression on people's faces when they looked her way. She didn't want to deal with it. As much as she hated to think about it, a small part of her secretly hoped that if she wasn't taking up all of Heather's free time, that maybe Heather would meet some nice guy. Maybe if Heather had a boyfriend, Andrea would be able to let her go.

Andrea knew of Heather's fear of heights so the only way she'd agree to go to the fair was if Heather would agree to ride the giant Ferris wheel with her. Heather agreed without hesitation.

Andrea was acutely aware of Heather's thigh resting against her own as they sat side by side on the Ferris wheel. She was painfully aroused but didn't dare move away. When the ride stopped with the two of them at the very top, Andrea assumed that it was to let some passengers on or off. It wasn't until about two full minutes later, when they still hadn't moved that she looked down at the man with the controls. He had a toolbox in one hand, and he was shouting something into the walkie-talkie in his other hand.

"What's happening?" Heather asked fearfully.

"It'll be okay. Don't worry." Andrea tried to reassure her.

Heather was starting to panic. She reached for Andrea's hand and scooted over even closer to her. Andrea was scared too, but it had nothing to do with the carnival ride. She wasn't sure she could contain her feelings any longer. The innocent touching was etching away at her resolve to control herself.

"Andie, I'm scared!" Heather pleaded.

When Andrea looked into Heather's eyes, it was all she could do to not take her in her arms and hold her, comfort her. It was then, that she saw something in Heather's eyes that she had never seen before. Whether it was real or not, Andrea didn't know. But it was there. It could have been that Andrea had wanted to see it so badly that she'd just imagined it. Her eyes drifted lower to Heather's beautiful full lips. Parted slightly, welcoming. Calling to her. She watched as Heather's breathing quickened. Yes, she was feeling it too.

Slowly, Andrea approached. She could feel Heather's hot breath against her face. She closed her eyes and was beginning to close the final inch between them when the ride suddenly jerked forward causing them to collide violently. The end result was a black eye for Andrea and a fat lip for Heather. They never talked about what almost happened that night.

When Andrea woke later that evening, she felt a little bit better. Her headache was gone, as was that horrible spinning feeling. She decided that what she needed to get over Heather was a good dose of Terri, which unfortunately couldn't happen until next weekend, but she decided to call her anyhow.

The phone was answered on the fourth ring.

"Hey, Ter!"

"Andrea!" Terri sounded very surprised to hear from her. "What's wrong?" she asked.

"Nothing's wrong. Why would you think that?" Andrea asked.

"Well, first of all, you never call me at home, and secondly, you didn't ask what I was wearing."

Andrea was silent on the other end of the phone. Terri was right. There was something wrong, but she couldn't talk about it.

"Andrea? Are you still there?"

"Yeah. Sorry. I just called to see if you'd be home next weekend."

"That depends. If you're planning to come home for a visit, I'll be home. If you're just asking out of curiosity, I'll be out."

"I was thinking about coming for a visit," Andrea said.

"Wonderful. Look I've got um ... *company* ... call me this week with your flight information and I'll pick you up at the airport."

"Okay, Ter. Have a good night."

"You sure you're okay, Reynolds? You don't seem like yourself," Terri noted again.

"I'm fine. See you next weekend, okay?" She hung up before Terri could ask any more questions. Besides the fact that she wasn't sure she could talk about this with Terri, she did not want to disrupt her evening.

Heather, dressed for work, was staring at Andrea's door, contemplating knocking on it. She was surprised that she had not left her room all day. She wanted to know whom Andrea had spent the night with. She couldn't, for the life of her, understand why she even cared, but she did. She was what? Curious? Jealous? No, it couldn't be jealous. What was the big deal anyway? Andie was attractive. No, she was more than attractive; she was gorgeous, compassionate, and apparently wealthy. She could have any woman she wanted.

After staring at the closed door for several minutes, Heather simply walked away. They hadn't really spoken since Andrea moved in, and if they did speak now, it would probably just turn into an argument, leaving Heather in a foul mood before work.

Chapter 7

Andrea felt nervous on the ride to work. She wasn't sure she could face Tammy, or Jamie, for that matter, after her drunken escapade on Saturday night. She had considered calling Tammy the night before, just to thank her again, but ended up falling asleep before she'd mustered up the courage.

Carlos was eagerly waiting for her as she approached the production area. He didn't look upset, but still she approached with caution. She had hoped for this to be a problem free day. She still felt a little bit hung over and was in no mood to deal with a crisis first thing in the morning.

"Good morning, Carlos," she said hesitantly.

He smiled, no longer able to contain his excitement.

"Andrea, I have some good news, but I can't discuss it with you here." He pulled her aside so that no one could overhear them. "Meet me at the diner up the road after work." He was beaming.

Andrea had never seen him act this way. She was skeptical. What was so important that he had to meet with her outside of work? And why was he so happy? Carlos was never happy.

"Okay, Carlos," she agreed casually. It wasn't as if she had anywhere else to be anyway.

As first break approached, she was pleased that she had successfully avoided even the slightest bit of contact with Tammy, but she sensed that once the horn sounded, Tammy would seek her out.

As predicted, just seconds later, she spotted Tammy and Jamie headed her way. *Guess I can't hide forever.*

"Good morning, ladies," she said with a hint of charm and cheeriness that she hoped sounded sincere.

"Hey, Andrea," Jamie said, and then abruptly added, "Gotta go," before she went traipsing off after some girl with short dark hair and a multitude of piercings.

Andrea and Tammy stood silently watching Jamie's desperate attempt at getting the other woman's attention.

"She'll never change," Tammy admitted with a sigh. Both women smiled and turned to face each other. The silence was uncomfortable. Andrea was the first to speak.

"Look … I … um … thanks again." *Brilliant Andrea. That's the best you could come up with.*

Tammy chuckled softly. "You're welcome. It was nice to have some company for a change."

"You don't date much do you?" Andrea knew the question was a bit personal but somehow the bond they shared compelled her to pry.

Tammy just shook her head no.

"Why not?" Andrea pressed on.

Tammy shrugged her shoulders, then, after a long pause replied, "Sometimes people spend their whole lives searching for the one thing that's been right there under their noses the whole time." As she said it, she looked over at Jamie. Andrea saw the longing in her eyes and realized that Tammy was in love with Jamie. Jamie apparently had no clue. Why hadn't she seen it before? She was usually more observant than that—then again, maybe she wasn't.

The horn sounded again signalling the end of their break but Andrea stopped Tammy before she could rush off.

"About that dinner I owe you … How's tomorrow night?"

"Sure," Tammy replied, smiling as she walked back to her workstation.

By the time Carlos arrived at the diner, Andrea had been waiting nearly forty-five minutes. She had started to think that he wasn't going to show up, and that maybe she should just go home. But go home and do what? Watch Rebecca and Heather be all lovey-dovey with each other. No way. She definitely needed to find something to do to occupy her evenings. Sure, she could hang out at the plant, but that was only inviting problems. She would undoubtedly end up stuck in the middle of someone else's troubles.

Maybe softball or beach volleyball. She'd played every sport she could while she was in school but hadn't been in one place long enough since then to join a team. Maybe now was the right time.

"Hey, Andrea! Sorry I'm late. I got stuck in a meeting," Carlos said as he sat down opposite her in the corner booth she had selected.

"No problem," she replied evenly, despite being a little bit angry. He could have at least called to tell her he'd be late.

The server took their orders immediately and as soon as she was gone, Andrea asked, "So what is so important that you couldn't tell me at the plant?"

"Do you know Jack Greene?" Carlos asked.

"Yeah. He's the Senior Launch Supervisor. What about him?"

"He gave his notice over the weekend. He's moving to Chicago to go take care of his elderly mother."

"So?" She wanted to know what this had to do with her. Sometimes getting information out of Carlos was like pulling teeth.

"When the team met this morning, they asked me if I thought you'd be a good fit as his replacement."

"Me? Why me? Don't they want to promote someone on the inside?"

"They want you. They've been hearing about the infamous Andrea Reynolds for years, and now that they've seen you in action, they want you on their team."

"Well, I'm flattered. But I'm not interested," she replied flatly.

"Not interested? Why not? The money's great. The hours are great. No more weekends. No more travelling. What more could you want?" He was astonished. He thought she'd jump at this chance.

"No offence, Carlos, but the sooner I get out of this town the better." Had things been different, she might have considered taking the job, but she knew she had to get away from Heather as soon as possible, which would never be soon enough. She still had four or five months to go before she was done here. Enough time to undo all the healing she had done.

"I thought you liked it here," he said with a grain of disappointment.

"It's not that I don't like it here. There's just some old history that seems to have caught up with me here."

"Did you run into an old girlfriend or something?"

"Something like that," she admitted freely. She had never discussed her personal life with Carlos, so she was a little bit shocked that he knew she was a lesbian. Not that it was a secret or anything. Andrea simply preferred to keep her personal life private.

Thankfully, their food arrived and Carlos seemed more interested in the fried chicken on his plate than Andrea's love life. Andrea, on the other hand, was feeling extremely guilty for ordering a clubhouse with fries and gravy. She should have ordered something healthier but the last few days had been difficult, and she hadn't had much of an appetite. So what, if she indulged a little now and then? She could benefit from gaining a pound or two, since her clothes were starting to fit a little bit loosely.

As they ate, they chatted casually about the weather and reminisced about the fun they'd had when they worked together at the plant in Mexico. The conversation remained light and friendly with no further mention of the job offer again until Carlos stood up to leave.

"Just think about it. Okay, Andrea?" He fished a twenty from his pocket and casually tossed in on the table to cover their bill.

Carlos was a good honest man and Andrea hated that he had vouched for her, and she was putting him an awkward position.

"I'll think about it, but don't get your hopes up, Carlos," Andrea said dejectedly.

He seemed so disappointed, but Andrea couldn't take this job just to appease Carlos, she had to do what was best for her.

Heather was furious. Her return flight had been delayed for four hours due to mechanical problems and she didn't get to bed until nearly five A.M. The constant beeping of Andrea's alarm clock, only two hours later, was enraging her.

Assuming Andrea had somehow forgotten to turn it off, and had already left for work, Heather stormed into Andrea's room ready to throw the damn thing against the wall.

"Just five more minutes," Andrea pleaded, oblivious to Heather's presence.

Heather's first instinct was to yell at her to get up, but something in her voice caused her to turn and look toward the bed.

"Andie? Are you okay?" There was no response from Andrea. For an instant, Heather thought that maybe Andrea had been out drinking again and that she was just hung over. When she flipped on the light, the sight she saw caused her to rush over to the bed. Andie's sheets and clothes were sweat-soaked and she was shivering.

"Andie?"

"Go away," Andrea muttered instinctively.

"You have to get out of these clothes."

"Go away. I have to get ready for work."

"You're not going anywhere. Stay put." Heather headed toward the bathroom and began to fill the tub, adjusting the temperature until the water was lukewarm.

While the tub was filling, Heather busied herself with finding dry clothes and clean sheets. It was both awkward and familiar looking through Andrea's things. There was a time when the two of them shared everything. They knew each other better than anyone else did; now, they really didn't know each other at all. Part of her felt like she was snooping through a stranger's drawers. Except that this stranger knew her deepest, darkest secrets—all but one of them. This stranger knew her hopes, her dreams, her desires; but she was a stranger nonetheless.

After finding a clean t-shirt and a pair of shorts, Heather had to stop herself from continuing to look through Andrea's things. She wanted to keep looking— to find clues as to who the adult Andrea was. Who did she love? Who loved her? What did she do in her spare time? Where had she been living all these years?

Stop it, Heather scolded herself and made her way back over to the bedside to find Andrea sound asleep again. She looked so peaceful that she hated to wake her, but she had to get out of those wet clothes.

"Andie?" she said softly, sitting gently on the bed.

"Go away!" Andrea didn't know who was trying to wake her up but she was tired and did not want to be bothered.

"Don't be so damn stubborn. Let me help you."

Andrea was having trouble focussing. The voice belonged to Heather, but what would Heather be doing in her room? She must be hallucinating.

"Andie, can you sit up?"

She watched as Andrea struggled to a sitting position. Heather wasn't sure whether her heart or her mind would win as the two of them wrestled for control over her actions. Her heart, although still broken, loved Andie more than anything in the world and wanted to take care of her, comfort her. Her mind, on the other hand, remembered the pain and wanted her to just walk away and leave Andrea to her suffering.

To make matters worse, there was still the undeniable fact that Andrea and Donna looked very much alike. Taking care of Andrea was reminiscent of caring for Donna for all those months. She wished for Rebecca or Justine to be home so that they could take care of her, but they weren't, so she was on her own.

Andrea started to lie back down and Heather reached out for her, grabbing her by the arm.

"Andie, you have to work with me here."

Heather pulled the covers back with her free hand and urged Andrea to swing her legs off the side of the bed.

"Cold ... So cold," Andrea said as she tried unsuccessfully to reach for the blanket.

"I know. Just a few more minutes. We're going to stand up now. Okay?"

Hopefully Andrea was strong enough to walk, because there was no way Heather could carry her. She counted "One ... Two ... Three."

As they stood, Andrea wavered and Heather had to wrap her arms around her in order to keep her from falling over. It was no use, Andrea's weight was too much for Heather to support, and both women went tumbling backward on the bed. Heather landed directly on top of Andrea.

For a moment, Heather forgot what she was even doing in Andrea's room. It felt so good—so right. It wasn't until Andie moaned and raised her hips to meet Heather's thigh that she even realized what she was doing. And what was she doing exactly? This was insanity, but she wanted it to continue. Andrea wasn't even lucid enough to understand what was happening. Her reaction was probably involuntary. That thought was almost too painful to consider. This had to stop now.

Heather abruptly stood up and somehow found the strength to pull Andrea up with her. Twenty-three small, slow, cautious steps later, she had managed to get Andrea seated on the edge of the tub. Now, there was just the little matter of her clothes to deal with. God help her, she didn't think she could handle seeing Andrea naked. It appeared as though she wouldn't have a choice as she watched Andrea struggle with her t-shirt, unable to pull it up over her head, nearly slipping off the tub in the process.

Okay, Heather, you can do this. She took a deep breath and knelt down in front of Andrea's shivering body. Grasping the bottom edge of the shirt, she slowly lifted it up and over Andrea's head, inadvertently brushing her fingers across her nipple in the process.

Oh, God! She was helpless to look away from the perfect breasts staring her in the face. So round. So full. So close.

"I'm going to be sick!" Andrea shouted, shoving Heather away in her haste to reach the toilet on the other side of the room.

Heather knew she had a weak stomach for these things and quickly got up and left the room, closing the door behind her. She stood patiently by the door listening to make sure Andrea was okay, all the while taking deep breaths, trying to squelch her body's involuntary response to the stimuli.

Andrea sat dumbfounded and exhausted on the bathroom floor. She thought Heather had been there with her, helping her, but she wasn't there. It must have been a dream. She didn't remember filling the tub, but maybe she had. Realizing, suddenly, why the tub was full in the first place, she made her way over to it and stepped in. She was freezing, and lowering herself into the cool water was the last thing she wanted to do, but she remembered her mother forcing her to get into a cool tub when she'd had a fever as a child.

Heather continued to listen from the other side of the bathroom door, hearing the gentle splashing of the water as Andrea got into the tub. She knew it wasn't safe to leave her in there alone for long, so she quickly made her way to her own room and riffled through the medicine cabinet until she found some Gravol and acetaminophen. She wasn't sure if Andrea had the flu or food poisoning but right now, it didn't matter. The Gravol would settle her stomach and the acetaminophen would help with the fever.

Once Heather returned, she listened carefully at the bathroom door again to make sure Andrea was all right. Confident that what she heard was Andrea washing her hair, she decided she had time to change the sheets before Andrea would be ready to get out of the tub. She was drawn instinctively to Andie's pillow. She buried her face in it, inhaling the familiar scent. Memories flooded her mind. How many times had she gone back to her room, hours after Andie had left, and held her pillow close, letting the intoxicating aroma that was uniquely Andie overwhelm her senses? Even now, it was comforting, and undeniably arousing.

"Heather?" Andie said as she exited the bathroom. Why was Heather in her room? Maybe she hadn't dreamt it after all.

"Andie, how do you feel?" She felt her face flush, having been caught with Andrea's pillow.

"What are you doing here?"

"You're sick. You had a really high fever."

"Yes, I know. But why are you here?"

Because I still love you, you big jackass is what she wanted to say, but she wasn't ready to admit that to Andrea yet.

"Your alarm clock kept ringing. So I came in to shut it off, and well … you were very sick." It was partially the truth. The alarm clock was her original motivation for going into Andie's room, but it wasn't why she stayed.

"Oh! Sorry." Andrea was disappointed. She'd hoped that Heather truly cared about her. That Heather was there to take care of her. To comfort her. The way she always had.

"I changed your sheets. Get back in bed while I go get you something to drink."

"I can't. I have to go to work."

"Andie, you can't go to work today, and you know it. Do you even know why you're sick?" Heather asked.

"Food poisoning, I guess. I had dinner at the diner yesterday, but I was feeling fine until I started puking around two o'clock." She was feeling better for a few minutes after her bath, but she was starting to feel sick again. The room was starting to spin, and she was having trouble focussing on Heather.

"Lay down, before you fall down," Heather said before rushing to the kitchen to get some ginger ale.

By the time she returned, Andrea was lying halfway across the bed with her feet still on the floor. Heather struggled with Andrea's limp body, but managed somehow, to get her situated properly in the bed. Aside from the fever, Andrea was probably severely dehydrated and Heather knew she had to wake her up again.

"Andie!" she whispered and pulled her up into a sitting position again. She seemed more coherent as she swallowed the offered pills and sipped slowly at her ginger ale.

Chapter 8

Several hours later, Andrea was awakened by the ringing of her cell phone. She groggily answered it and was pleased to hear Tammy's voice on the other end of the line. Tammy explained that several people at the plant had called in sick today because of food poisoning. Since they had a dinner date tonight, Tammy suggested that she would stop by in about half an hour with some soup for Andrea instead.

When Andrea greeted Tammy on the front porch, she was still wrapped in her heavy blanket, unable to shake the chills from her fever.

Heather, who had been sleeping on the couch when Andrea went out the door, was wide-awake when the two women entered the house.

"Hi, I'm Tammy," she said cheerfully. "I brought *sickie* here some soup."

"I'm sure you did," Heather replied sarcastically as she examined the woman standing before her, trying to find a flaw.

Andrea took notice of Heather's rude remark and ushered Tammy to the bedroom.

"I'll be right back," she told Tammy and returned to the living room to confront Heather.

"She's just a friend." Andrea did not know why she felt compelled to justify Tammy to Heather, but she did it never the less.

"I really don't care. It's none of my business."

"It sure sounds like you care," Andrea shot back.

"Did it? So sorry. Should I apologize to your little friend?" Heather asked, sarcasm dripping from every word.

"Don't bother," Andrea replied before storming back into her bedroom. Heather was acting like a child. It was none of her business who Andrea spent time with or why. She should be grateful that Andrea didn't need her to take care of her anymore.

"What's with her?" Tammy asked when Andrea returned.

"Your guess is as good as mine," Andrea replied. She honestly couldn't understand Heather's behaviour. She was obviously still angry over what Andrea had done, but that was between them. There was no need to take it out on her friends.

"How do you feel?"

"A bit better. I slept most of the day."

"Glad to hear it. I brought you chicken and rice." She pulled the bowl of soup out of the bag and placed it on the table in front of Andrea.

"Thanks," she said shyly. "You didn't have to do this, you know."

"I didn't have to … I wanted to. But you do realize that you still owe me dinner right?"

Heather waited anxiously for Rebecca to get home. Her earlier excitement from the innocent contact with Andie had not subsided. Just imagining what was going on in Andie's bedroom right now was filling her with an unpleasant mix of jealousy and arousal.

When Rebecca finally walked through the door, nearly an hour later, she was nearly attacked by Heather who flew into her arms and met her lips urgently.

"What's gotten into you?" a surprised Rebecca asked when she was able to break away from Heather's grasp for a moment.

"I need you … Right now!" Heather insisted.

"Can I at least go take a shower first?"

"I'll help," Heather replied before taking Rebecca's hand and dragging her into the bathroom.

Rebecca had no idea what was going on with Heather, but she was enjoying this way too much to care. Within seconds, she had stripped Rebecca's clothes and was feverishly removing her own. Rebecca was in awe. She didn't know what to expect from Heather. Although she was always a very playful and responsive lover, she rarely initiated sex and when she did, she was never this aggressive.

Heather was first to step under the spray of the shower. She reached between her own legs and opened herself to Rebecca as an invitation to join her. Rebecca was instantly aroused and wasted no time joining her under the steady stream of water. Their lips met with a fury; tongues battled for control.

When Heather's mouth moved south, taking Rebecca's left nipple between her lips, Rebecca struggled to maintain her balance. She was certain she was going to fall. If not because of the slippery floor than because of the fact that she was so light headed. She was certain she had never been this aroused in her life. Thankfully, Heather noticed her struggling and manoeuvred them backward so that Rebecca was leaning against the back wall of the shower stall.

Heather continued her assault on Rebecca's left nipple. Her fingers found their way to Rebecca's pulsating mound and slipped between the sensitive folds, gently grazing her hard clit. She looked up and grinned knowingly at Rebecca when she found the slick wet evidence of her arousal.

She licked her lips in anticipation and kissed her way down Rebecca's body until she reached the source of her sweet nectar. Her tongue teased and tormented the sensitive flesh until she felt Rebecca's orgasm nearing. She slipped two fingers inside and sucked the hard nub between her lips, gently teasing it with her teeth. Rebecca's body instantly went rigid and Heather struggled to maintain her hold on the source of her pleasure. Rebecca's orgasm was so powerful, Heather was certain she felt it through her body as well.

Rebecca was going to suggest that they continue this on the bed but the look on Heather's face told her that wasn't an option. As soon as she had recovered enough, she met Heather's hungry lips with her own and slipped her hand between them to meet the impatient thrusts of Heather's hips.

Heather was open, ready, and needed Rebecca inside her. She wrapped her legs around Rebecca's waist, opening herself even wider as Rebecca slipped two, then three fingers deep inside her. Fingers clasped behind Rebecca's neck, Heather arched her back and let her head fall back as she rode Rebecca's long strong fingers.

Rebecca felt the muscles tightening around her fingers and increased the speed of her thrusts knowing that Heather was close. Heather urgently flung her body forward meeting Rebecca's lips once again with her own as the first waves of her orgasm passed through her body. Pushing her thumb against Heather's clit in combination with one final deep thrust sent Heather over the edge. Rebecca felt the pain as Heather bit down on her shoulder at the height of her climax, but she didn't care. It was amazing to see Heather this way. Rarely did she let herself go like this.

Heather was insatiable. They had made love for several hours and yet Heather kept reaching for Rebecca trying to fill the void she was feeling. No matter how many times they made love, Heather was unable to satisfy the yearning she felt.

Rebecca was exhausted. It was after eleven and she just wanted to go to sleep.

"Heather, I can't ... I'm so tired."

Heather was frustrated but she understood. "I'm sorry," she said to the already sleeping Rebecca as she rose to put on a robe. She felt ashamed of herself for using Rebecca the way she had, and worse than that, it hadn't even worked. She was still hungry, still yearning.

Heather didn't understand what she was feeling. She couldn't believe her body had reacted so strongly to Andie, especially when she was still so angry with her. She thought maybe focussing on Rebecca would help get her mind off Andrea but that didn't work. How was she ever going to get past this?

She made herself a cup of tea and headed outside to get some air. The night air was crisp and cool. The sky was filled with bright stars and for a few moments, Heather was able to lose herself in the twinkling abyss. Nights like these were usually her favourites, but tonight, the vast canopy was making her feel small. In the grand scheme of it all, she was really inconsequential. Her problems weren't that bad. Her feelings for Andrea were merely an inconvenience. The feelings would pass.

Satisfied with her self-assessment, she made her way back into the house happily noticing that Tammy's car was gone. *Well, at least she didn't spend the night.*

Heather decided that avoiding Andrea wasn't helping to diminish her rekindled affection for the woman, so a new course of action was necessary. Andrea overload is what she called it. She would spend as much time with her as possible and maybe she would find out that Andrea had some bad habits or that she had developed some personality disorders that would make her less attractive.

It was finally Friday. Heather hadn't seen Andrea all week because of their conflicting schedules, but she had the weekend off and was determined to spend some time with her.

Heather was sitting in the living room, reading a magazine, when Andrea emerged from her bedroom with a large duffle bag over her shoulder.

"Going somewhere?" she asked nonchalantly.

"Actually, I'm going home for the weekend," Andrea replied, completely unaware of Heather's motives.

"Why?"

Andrea thought about her response for a few seconds before answering. Somehow, telling Heather that she was going home to get laid didn't have that much appeal.

"I have to pick up my mail," she replied. It was partially the truth.

"That's a long way to go to just pick up your mail."

"I'm also going to visit a friend." Andrea was getting frustrated with Heather's questioning. She was running late and whatever possessed Heather to start speaking to her today, after practically ignoring her since she'd arrived, would have to wait.

"A friend or a *friend*?" Heather asked hesitantly. She could tell Andrea was growing impatient, and she didn't think she wanted to hear the answer to the question. What if Andrea had a girlfriend back home? Would that change how she felt? Probably not. It would only complicate this already maddening situation, but it would explain why Andrea hadn't really paid any attention to her. Didn't Andie find her attractive anymore? Maybe that's what was really bothering her. Even though she didn't want to want Andie, she did; and she wanted Andie to want her.

"Does it matter?" Andrea asked, wondering why Heather picked this moment to delve into her personal life. She'd had over a month to ask these questions but couldn't be bothered before today.

Heather tried not to sound annoyed by Andrea's obvious deflection of the question.

"You know, I always hated it when you answered a question with a question."

"I know," Andrea replied as she headed out the door, leaving Heather to contemplate the response on her own.

Thanks to Heather's sudden need to chat, Andrea had to run through the airport and made it to the gate just in time for final boarding. Once she was comfortably settled into her window seat, she had time to process some of Heather's questions. She thought back to Tuesday and Heather's reaction to Tammy. She definitely seemed jealous, but why? Now, all the questions about why she was going home for the weekend.

Heather was with Rebecca, and after overhearing them in bed together the other night, she knew they were definitely not having any trouble in that regard. So why would Heather be jealous? Maybe it was time that they talked this out. If it didn't go well, then Andrea could move out. Anything had to be better than this.

Terri was definitely a welcome sight. Andrea spotted her immediately amongst the other people gathered around to greet their friends and family.

"Hi," she said as she gathered Terri in her arms and squeezed her tight, lifting her off her feet for a moment.

"Hey. I missed you too," Terri replied, stunned at the uncharacteristic greeting she received from Andrea, who appeared to be holding on to her for dear life. There was definitely something bothering her. Andrea was thin and she looked lost. She didn't seem to be the same cool confident woman Terri knew. She had always known Andrea was hiding something painful behind those steel-grey eyes but they never discussed it. It just wasn't their thing.

Terri knew that sometimes when Andrea touched her, she was really touching someone else. Someone she didn't talk about. But that was okay. That's how things were between them. No strings. No complications.

They did care about each other—there was no question about that. They simply enjoyed each other and kept things on a friendly level, rarely delving into each other's personal lives. Terri was genuinely concerned, but she wouldn't push too hard for information. She would not intentionally break their unspoken agreement. She enjoyed Andrea's company too much to potentially threaten their friendship.

They didn't speak much on the way to Terri's house. Andrea sat quietly in the passenger seat of Terri's brand new black Corvette taking in the scenery as if she was seeing it for the first time. She truly hated coming back to Cincinnati. There were too many memories. She showed no visible signs of a reaction when Terri unknowingly drove past the house Heather grew up in, but on the inside, she felt as though she was being ripped apart.

She wondered what caused Heather to be so chatty today. Since her arrival at the house several weeks ago, they'd had but the one conversation about Andrea moving out and that wasn't really a conversation at all. It was more of an exchange of information.

She closed her eyes and allowed the memory of the day she met Heather to fill her mind.

It was a warm spring day. She was in the second grade. It was recess. She hadn't paid much attention to the teacher earlier that morning when she introduced the new student who had just moved there from Virginia. When she saw Bobby McKinna shoving the new girl, whose name she didn't know because she hadn't bothered to pay attention, she felt the need to do something about it. She hated Bobby McKinna. He was the class bully.

Andrea watched as he poked the new girl with his chubby finger, yelling obscenities at her. The new girl was the smallest girl in the class. Her hair was pulled into pigtails, making her look even more innocent. Andrea usually never intervened when Bobby acted out. Since she bloodied his nose in kindergarten, he hadn't bothered with her and she hadn't bothered with him. She didn't really care about her other classmates; she was a loner. It was up to them to defend themselves so she didn't understand her sudden need to help the new girl.

She was just about to grab Bobby when the new girl suddenly kicked him in the shin and then punched him square in the nose. This new girl had spunk and Andrea was drawn to her instantly. He ran away crying, and although Andrea didn't know it then, she was in love.

"We're here," Terri said as she pulled into the driveway. "Are you awake?"

"Yeah. Sorry. I guess I nodded off for a minute." She lied. Terri didn't need to know what she was thinking.

As they walked through the front door of Terri's small but lavish home, Andrea smelled the wonderful aroma of her homemade lasagna.

"Lasagna?" she asked. It was her favourite meal and Terri was a great cook. Terri nodded and Andrea immediately rushed to the bedroom to put her duffle bag away.

When she returned, she saw the beautifully set dining room table with two place settings set perpendicular to each other facing out the huge picture window that overlooked Terri's immaculate gardens. She knew Terri couldn't afford the car she was driving, let alone this house, or most of the furnishings in it, on her receptionist's salary. She often wondered, but never asked. She had a good idea of how it was possible and it had to do with the other women in Terri's life, but that was okay.

Andrea was starting to feel better already. Terri always made her feel better. She made her feel safe and welcome. When she was with Terri, she was okay.

Andrea didn't know if Terri had brothers or sisters. She didn't know if Terri had lived there all her life. She didn't know if Terri had a criminal record, or if she had ever been married. What she did know, was that Terri's favourite singer was Joan Jett, that her favourite movie was Silence of the Lambs, and that she preferred Coke to Pepsi. That's all she needed to know. It worked for them.

Terri made her way from the kitchen with the bubbly lasagna, a large glass of milk for Andrea, and a glass of wine for herself. Terri knew that Andrea rarely drank alcohol, that she read a lot, and that her favourite colour was blue. That's all she knew about Andrea. That's all she needed to know.

The silence between them was uncomfortable. Although they never discussed anything of consequence, they always found something to talk about. Terri finally looked up from her half-eaten dinner and asked, "Do you want to talk about it?"

"About what?" Andrea replied, knowing what Terri meant, but hoping she would drop the subject.

"Let's start with why you haven't been eating lately. You've lost at least fifteen pounds since I saw you last."

More like twenty, Andrea thought before answering.

"I've been busy. And I can't seem to get used to all the fried foods down there," she replied. "I had a bout of food poisoning earlier this week too," she added hoping that would explain her dramatic weight loss to Terri.

"Try again, Reynolds." Terri wasn't falling for Andrea's lame excuses. "Food poisoning didn't cause this, and you love to cook. From what I hear, things are going extremely well at the plant, so what is keeping you so busy that you don't have time to eat?"

"I'm fine, Ter. Don't worry about me, okay." She lied.

Andrea was anything but fine. She couldn't eat and couldn't sleep. Living in the same house with Heather was slowly killing her. All week she'd been trying to shake a dream she had of Heather lying on top of her in her bed. She couldn't get it out of her mind. It seemed so real. Felt so right. Their bodies fit together perfectly. She could still feel Heather's firm breasts pressing against hers through the thin fabric of their t-shirts. She was amazed at how real the dream seemed and could think of little else all week. All she wanted to do was spend a few days drowning in Terri so that maybe her life would regain some sense of normalcy.

"I'll let it go for now. But you know I'm here for you if you want to talk about anything." There was little else Terri could do but offer to listen. Andrea was not going to tell her what was bothering her, so rather than argue about it, she decided to enjoy the few precious days they had together.

"Delicious as always, Ter," Andrea said as she rose from the table to carry their dirty dishes to the sink.

She was filling the sink with warm soapy water when Terri appeared behind her and wrapped her arms around her waist. Terri was shocked at the tension she felt in Andrea's body. This woman was going to explode.

"Hey," she said softly, "Leave those dishes to soak, go to the bedroom, and get naked for me. I'll be there in a couple of minutes."

Andrea wasn't about to argue with her. Andrea didn't usually argue with any woman who asked her to get naked.

Terri quickly retrieved a large bottle of sweet almond oil and poured a suitable amount into a smaller bottle. She added a small amount of cedar wood oil, jasmine oil, and sweet orange oil before mixing the concoction well. She filled a mug with hot water and placed the bottle in the hot water to warm gently. Her previous career as a masseuse had its share of benefits. She knew exactly what to do to relax Andrea. The only down side was that she'd probably fall asleep. But that was okay. She looked tired.

Terri heard the shower running as expected despite the fact that she knew Andrea had showered just before heading to the airport only a few hours earlier. Andrea was a bit obsessive about showering. It was an obsession Terri appreciated but also found a bit irritating. Sometimes it was okay to have sex first and shower after.

She took a thick oversized terrycloth bath towel and laid it on the bed. She lit the three lemongrass candles on the nightstand, turned off the lights, and changed into something more comfortable and less likely to be stained by the oil. Sure, she could do this naked, but that might be too much for her to handle.

Chapter 9

Andrea emerged from the bathroom a few minutes later wearing a t-shirt. She looked around the room wondering what Terri was up to this time.

"Hey, I thought I told you to get naked. Why are you wearing a t-shirt?" Terri asked.

"You mean this t-shirt?" Andrea asked as she pulled it up and over her head.

"That's better."

Terri struggled to keep her mind on the task at hand. She was losing the battle. The sight of Andrea's naked perfection was causing all sorts of unexpected, but not necessarily unwelcome reactions in her body.

"Get on the bed and lay on your stomach," Terri said with authority, willing her mind to think of anything but sex right now.

Andrea did as she was told. She trusted Terri completely and had never regretted it. Once she was comfortable, Terri pulled a sheet over Andrea legs to keep her warm. Then, she kneeled over Andrea, one knee on either side of her hips, and began pouring the warm oil over Andrea's back. She began at her shoulders with deep penetrating circles. Her efforts were rewarded by Andrea's moaning.

Andrea had no idea what Terri's plans were for the evening, but so far, so good. As Terri's strong, but graceful hands continued their path down her back, she forgot all, but what was going on right that minute. Right now, there was no Heather. There was only Terri and her magical hands.

Andrea was asleep in minutes and Terri was content just to sit next to her and watch her sleep for close to an hour. She looked so peaceful when she was sleeping. She wondered if Andrea would ever tell her what was causing her so much stress.

The bedside clock read 3:17 in bright red numbers and Andrea tried to gain her bearings after waking up in a strange bed. It took only a second to realize it was Terri sleeping next to her and to remember what happened last night. For the second time in two weeks, Andrea had passed out on someone. First Tammy, now Terri. *What is wrong with me?* She thought about waking Terri but it didn't seem right.

Andrea felt wonderful but was restless. Whatever Terri did to her last night took care of the nagging kink she'd had in her neck all week. She had no idea what time she fell asleep, but she felt completely rested and she knew Terri wouldn't wake up for at least three more hours. Her mind started to wander again and she fixated on the day Heather came to her house after school.

They were in the eighth grade. Heather had been pestering her about it since they first met and Andrea had always come up with excuses to keep Heather from seeing what went on in her house. She was ashamed. She was also scared. What if Heather started treating her differently because of it? She wouldn't be able to handle it if Heather stopped being her friend.

She remembered it like it was yesterday. It was her thirteenth birthday, but she didn't celebrate her birthday anyway. Her mother was always at work and her father just didn't care.

The minute they walked through the door, Andrea's father started yelling for his dinner from his usual spot in the living room—his big, brown recliner that he rarely got up from. The area around the chair was littered with empty beer cans.

Andrea knew what to expect from her father, and expected Heather to walk out and run home, but she didn't. She looked at Andrea compassionately, as if suddenly understanding why she had not ever been to the house before.

Andrea led her to the kitchen, where they quickly prepared a plate of spaghetti for him. She grabbed a fresh beer from the fridge and headed to the living room to hand him his meal.

Not two minutes later, the entire plate of food was sent careening across the cheap linoleum floor towards the kitchen.

"You call this food?" he shouted from his big brown chair. "Clean that up."

Andrea was embarrassed. She couldn't meet Heather's eyes. She stood dumbfounded as Heather silently began cleaning up the mess. Why is she doing this? She couldn't believe Heather hadn't run away crying after witnessing her father's outburst.

After they finished cleaning up Heather said, "Come on, let's go. I left your birthday present at my house."

Again, she was shocked and puzzled by Heather's kindness.

Two hours later, she was sitting at Heather's kitchen table, blowing out candles on a plate of cupcakes while Heather's parents sang happy birthday to her. It was all she could do to hold back the tears. From that moment on, Heather's parents became her parents.

Heather never did ask to go back to Andrea's house and Andrea never invited her again. The incident was never discussed. It was around that time that Andrea started feeling differently toward Heather. She couldn't put names to the feelings at the time, but she knew that she wanted to be around Heather all the time. When they weren't together, which was a rare occasion, she'd think about her constantly. She began sleeping at Heather's house more than at her own. Her own mother too busy to care; her father just didn't.

By six o'clock, Andrea was compelled to do something. Anything, to keep her mind from wandering to Heather again. She decided to make pancakes for breakfast.

When she returned to the bedroom, half an hour later, with pancakes and orange juice, Terri was still asleep. She sat on the edge of the bed and gently caressed Terri's beautiful face. Terri lazily opened her eyes and smiled.

"What time is it?" she asked her voice still raw with sleep.

Andrea found this extremely sexy and thought about doing away with the pancakes altogether.

"Six-thirty."

"You made breakfast?" Terri asked.

"Why do you sound so surprised?"

"It's early. You're usually still asleep when I get up," Terri said as she sat up, her blanket dropping to rest in her lap, revealing a simple black silk nightie that allowed more than a peek at her ample breasts.

She caught Andrea staring and smiled as she accepted the offered plate of pancakes and began to eat.

"What do you want to do today?" Terri asked.

"Your wish is my command. I have an appointment Monday morning before I fly out and I would like to take you shopping … maybe a nice Armani suit. Other than that, I have no plans."

"I think I should take you shopping. Your clothes fit so loosely now, I'd have a hard time imagining what was under them if I didn't already know." Terri put their plates aside, reached her hand under Andrea's t-shirt, and ran her fingertips seductively up and down the valley between her breasts.

"If you keep that up, neither of us will be getting new clothes today," Andrea said shakily. Terri's magical hands were working wonders once again.

"I'm sorry I fell asleep last night."

"Don't be. I expected it." Terri continued her teasing, dipping her hand lower with every stroke until she found her target. "It hasn't escaped my notice though, that you've been here for twelve hours and haven't kissed me yet," Terri said.

"I haven't?" Andrea asked thoughtfully, trying to remember if that was indeed the case.

"Hmm," she said as she leaned closer to Terri, their lips nearly touching. "Let me remedy that situation right away." She closed the distance between them and their lips met tenderly. A slow, sweet kiss. Andrea ran her fingers through Terri's short, blond, sleep-tousled hair and gently pulled away from the kiss.

"That was nice," Terri said languidly. "Are there more where that came from, or am I only going to get the one?"

"There will be plenty more … when I get out of the shower." She kissed the top of Terri's head before getting up.

"Seeing as you're not a big fan of shower sex, how 'bout I promise to behave myself and join you?" Terri stood, held Andrea's hands, looked deeply into her eyes, and saw nothing as usual.

"All in the interest of efficiency of course," Terri added and smiled mischievously.

"Well … in the interest of efficiency, I guess that would be okay. Not to mention the water conservation." Andrea was smiling now too. Her problems seemed miles away again and there was just her and this amazing woman who had the ability to heal her invisible wounds.

Minutes later, they didn't bother to get dressed before heading directly back to bed. Andrea gasped as her naked body made contact with Terri's. The sensation was amazing. It had been a long time since she'd been with anyone; in fact, she hadn't been with anyone since Terri about a month ago. Way too long by her standards. No wonder she was getting all worked up about Heather.

They kissed passionately, Terri's tongue demanding entry. When Terri pressed her fingers gently against Andrea's throat, Andrea knew the signal. Andrea knew all of Terri's signals, and there were many of them. If by chance, she happened to forget what one of the signals meant Terri would not hesitate to remind her.

Andrea pulled away from the kiss and looked into Terri's eyes to make sure she hadn't misread the signal. She hadn't, and that both excited her and scared her at the same time. She rested her right elbow firmly on the mattress supporting most of her weight and let her forearm lie gently on Terri's throat. She would not apply pressure. It was up to Terri how little or how much pressure she wanted to apply and she could do so by lifting her head.

Her tongue traced a path from her neck to her breasts, circling Terri's erect nipple with practiced patience. She rolled her right nipple between her thumb and index finger, gently tugging the engorged nub. Terri moaned and squeezed Andrea's left shoulder. Andrea recognized the signal and squeezed harder as she took as much of Terri's breast as possible into her mouth, savouring her taste, wanting to consume her. She licked, flicked, and sucked until she'd had her fill. Terri's body arching into her touch, conveying the pleasure she was feeling.

Her fingers lightly traced a path from her breast to the delicate flesh of Terri's inner thighs, teasing her with maddeningly light caresses until she could take no more. She smoothed the palm of her hand over Terri's pulsating mound, relishing in the slick wet juices that welcomed her.

Terri's finger made its way into her mouth. Yet another signal. As she sucked on Terri's long slender finger, she gently slipped inside her. Long, slow thrusts. She felt the muscles constricting around her fingers as Terri once again squeezed her left shoulder.

She increased the speed and force of her thrusts until Terri was writhing beneath her, gasping for air as her orgasm ravaged her body.

Andrea was powerless to fight her own building orgasm. She strained desperately against Terri's thigh and came the instant Terri's hand intervened.

"Oh God! Shit!" Andrea exclaimed. "I'm sorry." She had tried to fight it—to prolong it. It was hopeless.

"What's her name, Reynolds?" Terri asked directly, but in a non-accusatory tone.

"What are you talking about?" Andrea pleaded ignorance. She did not want to have this discussion; especially not right now.

"You're usually good for at least a half hour. So tell me, what is the name of the woman who has you so worked up?"

"It's been a while. That's all." It had been a while.

"Well, whatever her name is, she doesn't know what she's missing," Terri conceded as she pulled Andrea close to her and gently stroked her face until sleep consumed them.

"Have a good morning," Andrea said sincerely as Terri, looking stunning in the custom tailored Armani, three-button, chalk striped pantsuit Andrea bought her the day before, stepped out of the car and handed her the keys.

"Don't hurt my car, Reynolds," she said, only partially teasing. She was a bit afraid that Andrea might let out some of her aggression while driving. Despite spending their entire Saturday in bed, Andrea still seemed restless and that scared her.

"Don't you trust me, baby?" Andrea was toying with her now and she knew it.

"Just be careful. I'll see you for lunch right?"

"I'll be here," Andrea replied, waved, and squealed the tires for effect, as she pulled out of the parking lot at Cinci-Plastics.

Andrea had four hours to kill. The only thing she had to do was pick up her mail and go to the DMV to renew her driver's licence since it would expire on her birthday this weekend.

She eased into a large parking space in the tiny post office lot, scared to death of putting even the tiniest scratch on Terri's new car. She waited patiently, as an elderly woman with nearly blue hair struggled with the key to her post office box, blocking Andrea's path to hers.

"Dear, could you help me please? My eyes aren't quite what they used to be," the elderly woman asked.

Andrea took the key from the woman and opened the box without incident. She waited patiently while the woman retrieved her mail, one piece at a time, and shuffled over to a tabletop on which she could sort it. Andrea hadn't been exposed to many elderly people in her life so she often felt frustrated by them. She was so used to being independent, that she couldn't fathom not being able to do things for herself. She hoped that she would be spared the indignity of growing old and helpless. If it were up to her, she would die around age sixty-five. Earlier, if she was in poor health.

Andrea quickly sorted through her mail, throwing three quarters of it in the recycling bin. Wasn't it enough to get junk e-mail? *Apparently not*, she thought as she tossed in flyers offering great deals on new roofs with fifty-year warranties, low rate mortgages and a spectacular ad telling her to relieve her family of the stress of dealing with her funeral by pre-planning and paying for it in monthly instalments.

She found the envelope from the DMV, opened it and filled in the required information before leaving the post office. Traffic was light and she made it across town in record time. She quickly checked her appearance in the rear-view mirror before heading inside to renew her driver's licence.

The line was long. It seemed as though everyone picked this particular Monday morning to handle his or her business at the DMV. She reluctantly peeled off the next available number and took a seat, noting that they were currently calling out number eighty-three. She was number ninety-eight. Under different circumstances, she would simply leave and come back another time, but she did not have the luxury of options today. Her flight left at two-thirty, giving her just enough time to enjoy a quick lunch with Terri before catching a cab to the airport.

She watched as an endless stream of expressionless people inched forward in line as if they were headed to a gas chamber. Irate individuals raised their voices, unhappy that unpaid parking tickets, which they seemed to have no recollection of, were impeding their ability to renew their licence. Andrea was amazed at the number of people who apparently took no responsibility for their actions. How could they go through life as if their actions had no consequences?

About an hour and a half later, Andrea was sitting in the car in the parking lot. It was just after ten o'clock. It felt strange being in this city that she had a love-hate relationship with. When she left eight years ago, she had never dreamed of coming back. She left the memories, the pain, and the city behind. Although she'd returned regularly for visits during the last couple of years, seeing Heather again refreshed the memories she had buried. The details, as painful as they might be, were crystal clear. She dialed the number for her therapist and was astounded to hear that she could come right in.

Dr. Cochran was a short, stocky woman with sandy brown hair. Her office décor was minimalistic. She explained that too many patients were distracted by paintings or nick-knacks. "Uncluttered space helps unclutter the mind," she'd say to anyone who asked about her decorating style.

After forty-five minutes, Andrea left the office with a very cluttered mind. Dr. Cochran suggested that perhaps Andrea was angry with Heather for not telling her how she felt. Maybe she blamed Heather. Heather's inaction, causing Andrea's reaction. That Heather was somehow responsible for Andrea leaving. It was all nonsense as far as Andrea was concerned. She was not angry with Heather, she was angry with herself. The only thing Dr. Cochran did say that seemed logical to Andrea was that she and Heather needed to discuss the incident. They could not pretend it did not happen. They had to acknowledge it before they could move past it.

It was a beautiful late summer day. Fall was just around the corner. The sun was shining and the air was a comfortable sixty-five degrees. Deciding she did not want to be cooped up in a restaurant for lunch, Andrea stopped by her favourite Deli and picked up soup and sandwiches before returning to Cinci-Plastics.

Chapter 10

Andrea still had some time to kill, but she thought Terri might be worried about her car, so she decided to head over there early. Maybe she'd get the opportunity to meet with Mr. Crowley before lunch with Terri.

She knew Terri could see the parking lot from her desk, so Andrea was extra cautious when she pulled into the parking space. She had made it this far without putting a scratch on it; it would be terrible if something happened to it now, especially with Terri watching.

"You're early!" Terri said after glancing at the clock on her desk, which read eleven-fifteen.

"And you're beautiful!" Andrea replied after making sure no one could overhear her. She watched in awe as a blush crept across Terri's face, unsure of how a woman so beautiful could be embarrassed by the truth.

"I thought I'd check in with Lorraine and Mr. Crowley while I was here."

"I'll let him know you're here. You're on your own to find Lorraine though."

Andrea watched as Terri's talented fingers dialed Mr. Crowley's extension.

"He'll be out it a minute."

"Thanks. I picked up lunch at the Deli. I don't feel like sitting in a crowded restaurant today."

"You want to drive down to the river? We haven't done that in forever," Terri suggested.

"Sounds good." She looked over Terri's shoulder at Mr. Crowley who was heading their way.

"Hello, Mr. Crowley."

"Andrea! What a nice surprise. I had no idea you'd be in town. How long are you staying?"

"Actually, I'm heading back this afternoon, sir. I had some personal matters to take care of this weekend." She glanced over at Terri who was beet-red. "I just stopped in to say hello and make sure everything was going well."

She felt Terri's gaze on her back as she followed Mr. Crowley down the long hallway to his lavish corner office. He was a tall, thin man who took pride in his appearance. He was always impeccably dressed in fine suits and he still sported a full head of white hair. He jogged daily and was in remarkable shape for his sixty-eight years.

After exchanging pleasantries, Andrea decided to tell Mr. Crowley about the job offer she received from the plant in North Carolina. She knew she wouldn't accept the position, but the way rumours spread, there was no doubt word would get to Mr. Crowley before long. She didn't want him to think she was leaving.

"If it's about money, Andrea, I could offer you a little bit more, but not much. I'm no match for a big corporation like that."

"Sir, I'm not taking the position. I just wanted you to be aware of it in case word got around. I wanted to be upfront about it."

"Well, I'm happy to hear it. Not that I'm surprised—I've been waiting for someone to steal you away from us for a while now."

"I'm not going anywhere for the time being, except to find Lorraine." She stood and extended her hand. He looked her in the eye and shook her hand with enthusiasm, seemingly relieved that she wasn't leaving or asking for an increase in pay.

"It was nice to see you, Andrea. Keep up the good work."

"Always, sir."

She exited his office, headed down the long hallway, and winked at Terri on the way into the plant. She plucked a pair of safety goggles out of the bin and began her search for Lorraine.

Lorraine wasn't in her office and none of her staff seemed to know exactly where she was, so she walked the aisles, peering between boxes and equipment, ducking the path of forklifts until she found her. She was stuck in a corner, almost hidden behind a wall of boxes. Lorraine appeared almost frantic as she sorted through the boxes of parts, apparently rejecting about ninety percent of them for defects.

"Want some help?" Andrea asked after checking her watch. She still had twenty-five minutes. "I've got about half an hour." She really didn't mind helping. Maybe Lorraine would be a bit nicer to her in the future.

Lorraine looked at her questioningly. "Why?"

"Nothing better to do. What are we looking for?"

"I need to find at least one hundred good ones to ship out in an hour. Most of them have sink marks the size of Texas. I don't know how they missed this."

Sink marks were indentations in what was supposed to be a flat surface. Usually once the defect was detected, a technician would make changes to the process to correct the problem.

"Apparently the chiller clicked off sometime during the night shift and nobody caught it," Lorraine said in disgust as she continued tossing rejected parts into a bin.

A chiller was used to cool the water running through the mold. The molten plastic would take shape and hold its shape if the temperature was cool enough. If not, certain hot spots within the mold, or particularly thick sections of the plastic part would shrink and set at a different rate than the rest of the part causing a sink mark.

"Don't the auditors check that every two hours?" Andrea asked, although the obvious answer was yes, which no doubt compounded Lorraine's mood. One of her staff had somehow neglected their duties last night.

"Yes." She did not expand. She did not want to confess to Andrea that some of her staff members were new and in training. Andrea would be all over her, wanting to check the parts being shipped to North Carolina.

"I hear things are going well at the plant," Lorraine said in an attempt to deflect the scrutiny she felt any time Andrea was around.

"It's been good. No problems to speak of." Andrea suddenly was finding more good parts than bad ones. "Hey, the problem must have started with this box."

Lorraine sorted through the boxes and was pleased to find that the parts produced before the box Andrea was sorting were acceptable. She had more than enough parts to make her shipment.

"Thanks."

"No problem." Andrea looked at her watch and realized that it was nearly noon.

"Take it easy. It's not worth getting all stressed out about." Although the sentiment was genuine, the words were meaningless to Lorraine. Through her years, Andrea had yet to meet a Quality Manager who wasn't stressed out all the time.

She walked away with a better understanding of the daily stresses that Lorraine faced. She hoped Lorraine was left with the feeling that Andrea's constant badgering and double-checking was a well-meant attempt to help. She never harassed Lorraine for the sake of harassing her; she just wanted to make sure she was on top of things. Maybe if they each gave in a little bit, their strained relationship would be a little bit better off.

Terri was sitting at her desk, staring at the clock when Andrea made her way back to the reception area. Andrea had stopped to freshen up in the bathroom in the plant and ended up getting involved in a discussion about her beloved Bengals. Football was one topic Andrea could talk about for hours.

"Now, you're late," Terri said in a flat tone.

"And you're still beautiful."

They both smiled and headed to the car, happy that they had this time together but sad that it would soon be coming to an end. The drive to and from the river would take up half of Terri's one hour lunch break, but there wouldn't be too many more beautiful sunny days to enjoy.

As they drove to a remote parking area along the banks of the Ohio River, Andrea felt a strange mixture of sadness and anxiety. Being at the river reminded her of the times she and Heather would spend their evenings sitting out there. Although she had been there with Terri a few times, it just wasn't the same. She had always thought of this as her and Heather's special place. Being there with Terri seemed almost wrong.

She was also apprehensive about heading back to Heather's that afternoon. She had managed to keep most of her thoughts of Heather at bay while she was with Terri. Soon she'd be returning to a place where she'd be unable to escape Heather. Every day was a new challenge. She had gotten used to Heather ignoring her as if she wasn't even there, but the day she left, Heather had asked all those questions. Was Heather expecting them to be friends now, or was she just being nosy?

"Why so quiet?" Terri asked between bites of her sandwich. She knew she wouldn't get an answer from Andrea, but she asked anyway.

"Just wishing I could stay longer," Andrea replied. In a way, that was the truth. Terri was the only person who could help her forget Heather, even if it was for just a few minutes at a time. What she wouldn't give to stay for even a few hours longer.

"Me too. I hate that you're so far away. Not that you're ever close by, but usually you're not gone for so long."

"I know. Things are going well though, so maybe I can come back more often. It's not like I have anything else to do, especially on the weekends," she replied dejectedly. Any time she wasn't at the plant was pure torture. She wasn't sure if it was easier to watch Rebecca be affectionate toward Heather, or to not be able to see them and only speculate as to what they were doing.

She thought it would be easier while Heather was at work, but when she was gone, Andrea longed to be near her—even if Rebecca was with her. The situation was hopeless. She didn't want to be near her, but she couldn't stand to be away.

"You really don't like it there, do you?" Terri asked sympathetically.

She met Terri's eyes and replied, "It's complicated. I can't explain it."

"Can't or won't?"

"Won't," she replied and glanced at her watch. "We should get going so you're not late." Andrea was sure Mr. Crowley suspected there was something going on between the two of them so she didn't want to give him any reason to give Terri a hard time about it. One thing he despised was tardiness.

On the way back to the car, Andrea stole a glance at an old rusty shack about a quarter-mile down the river—it was her shack—her secret hideaway. That was where she went to be alone. Not even Heather knew about it. As her feelings for Heather grew, she'd go there more frequently until it almost became a second home. Those long nights when she couldn't stay home, but couldn't handle being so close to Heather, she'd hide out there. The shack was abandoned and each time Andrea went, she'd bring a few things with her to make it more like home.

She had a makeshift bed made from an old inflatable air mattress and a few blankets she'd snuck out of her house. Since she did all of the laundry, no one would ever notice them missing.

She had a small radio and several flashlights for those long nights when she didn't bother going home at all. She kept a photo album, filled with pictures of her mother and Heather, hidden away along with a box filled with numerous love-letters she'd written to Heather over the years. She'd never found the courage to give them to her. *Too late now.*

When they arrived at the car, Andrea took one more look and wondered if those things were still in there or if someone had come along and taken them. With the sweltering summer heat and the incredibly humid air, there was a good chance that even if they were still there, they'd be damaged beyond recognition. Maybe one day, when she was there alone, she'd take the time to check it out.

As soon as her flight took off, that nagging kink in Andrea's neck returned. Living in the same house with Heather was definitely going to kill her if something didn't change. Maybe Heather was feeling the same way. Maybe her intrusive questions the other day were her way of reaching out. Had she had more time that day, she definitely would have taken the time to sit and talk with her.

Meeting with Dr. Cochran only highlighted the need for the two of them to open the lines of communication. Andrea agreed with that wholeheartedly, but what she didn't agree with was that, somehow deep down, she blamed Heather for what happened. Looking back on it now, Heather did make her feelings known. Andrea was just too afraid to acknowledge them.

Eight years wasted, for what? Fear?

Chapter 11

Heather busted through the front door, discarding her sweat-soaked clothes on the floor. Thinking no one was home, she was enjoying the sensation of the cool air-conditioned air as it tingled against her over-heated skin.

She had waited for Andie to come home the night before and when she didn't, she was consumed with jealousy. That afternoon, when Andie still hadn't arrived home, Heather grew even more restless. Her solution was to go for a long jog and try to clear her mind.

Andrea stopped dead in her tracks when she unknowingly swung the kitchen door open and found herself face to face with the naked Heather.

Heather's natural instincts would have been to cover up, but Andrea was looking at her as if she had never seen a naked woman before. She felt cherished, and adored; not the least bit uncomfortable, although completely exposed and vulnerable.

Andrea felt the tightness in her chest and realized she wasn't breathing. Heather was a goddess. Her sun-bronzed skin, glistening with sweat, looked so soft and smooth, she just wanted to reach out and touch it. She had a small patch of light hair the size of a silver dollar to serve as a reminder that she was indeed a natural blonde. Her breasts were firm and full. She watched them rise and fall as Heather struggled to draw air into her still-recovering lungs.

"I didn't think anyone was home," Heather said through ragged breaths, her eyes fixated on Andrea's face.

"I parked out back. Had to wash my car." She struggled with every word. Her mind was unable to focus on anything except the most beautiful creature standing before her.

Andrea stood for several minutes taking in the beautiful sight before forcing her body to do the one thing it didn't want to do. Her gaze never wavered from Heather's beauty as she blindly walked over to the couch and retrieved the throw blanket from its usual location.

Slowly, she walked over to Heather, every movement a conscious struggle between right and wrong. Draping the blanket around Heather's shoulders was the last thing she wanted to do. She could have stayed right where she was and just taken in Heather's womanly curves all day. She convinced herself that covering her up was the right thing to do despite what her body was telling her.

She was careful not to touch Heather as she wrapped the blanket around her shoulders and pulled it closed in front of her.

"We don't need you catching a cold now, do we?" she said as coolly as possible before forcing her feet to move away.

Heather was left standing dumbfounded in the living room as Andrea retreated to the safety of her bedroom. She could not believe that Andrea walked away. It was just like when they were teenagers again and Heather was trying to get a reaction from Andrea.

She would purposely strip naked in front of Andrea any time she had to change her clothes. She would even walk over to where Andrea was sitting or standing and start talking to her, her naked body only inches away. It was all in an effort to get a reaction. Andrea never reacted then, and she didn't react today. Heather felt the tears welling up in her eyes as she picked her clothes up off the floor and headed for the shower.

Andrea sat on the bed, taking deep breaths, willing her body to relax. She was painfully aroused. She had only been home an hour, and already, she was as worked up as before she'd gone to visit Terri. She stood up, locked the door, and made herself comfortable on the bed. Visions of Heather, past and present, filled her mind as she fantasized that it was Heather's hand travelling the length of her body—diving into her deep wet recesses, stroking her engorged clit, straining to bring her the relief she sought. Her body shuddered and rose involuntarily from the bed as she ascended into oblivion before collapsing once again, exhausted. The tears came quickly, and she did not try to fight them as she cried herself to sleep.

Heather allowed the cool mist of water wash away the tears, but it did nothing to wash away the pain. The realization that Andie did not want her was almost more painful than what she had felt when she walked away eight years ago and never looked back. If Andrea had only touched her, she was certain she would have disintegrated in her arms. She wanted so badly to be loved by her. When the reality that she wouldn't finally sank in, it was almost unbearable. Maybe it would be best for her if Andrea did move out. First, she had to know why Andie left her. Once she understood that, maybe she could let it go.

Terri looked curiously at a small slip of paper that was taunting her from where it rested on the floor mat. She didn't remember seeing it earlier when she drove down to the river with Andrea.

As she parked her car in the driveway, she reached down and picked up the crumpled piece of paper, certain that it contained an important clue as to what Andrea was doing earlier that morning.

She carefully opened the crumpled remains and examined its contents. It was a receipt for a licence renewal from the DMV. Immediately, Terri's powers of deduction took over, and she concluded that usually people renewed their driver's licence just before their birthdays. Therefore, Andrea's birthday must be soon.

Tomorrow, she would set out on a fact-finding mission. She knew that Andrea didn't have a personnel file, since she wasn't an employee, but she thought that at some point they might have needed Andrea's birth date to arrange her travel abroad.

It was Thursday evening and Andrea had avoided any contact with Heather since their uncomfortable encounter on Monday. She sat outside watching the dark ominous clouds gathering overhead as the smooth, soulful sounds of Van Morrison, playing on a nearby boom box, soothed her.

For once, the weatherman had been right. It was going to be a good storm; Andrea could feel it in her bones. Her body was alive and humming as the wind picked up and danced with the trees.

The sweet smell of rain permeated her senses. Eyes closed, she raised her face to allow the wind and rain to caress her. Nothing made her feel more alive than a good thunderstorm. The hairs on her arms stood up, reacting to the electrical current floating in the air.

Heather was weary of storms. They scared her. They were manic and unpredictable. *A lot like Andie,* she thought as she looked out her window at Andrea sitting there enjoying the storm. She knew, despite her fear, that it was now or never. She hadn't been able to catch up with her all week, and she wanted to take Andie out for dinner on her birthday this Sunday. She didn't think Andie would have any plans, since she didn't appear to know many people in town. Besides that, she hadn't yet had a chance to thank her for the watch, and they needed to talk. If they were ever going to get past this, they had to talk about it and dinner would be an opportune time.

Heather pulled a hooded sweatshirt over her torso and ventured out into the wind and rain. If Andrea was surprised by her presence, she didn't show it. She didn't even turn her head to look at her.

"Hey," Andrea said as casually as possible, her heartbeat quickening as Heather approached.

"Hey, yourself," she replied, taking a seat in the empty chair next to Andrea, who still hadn't looked at her.

"I'm sorry if I'm interrupting your alone time."

"You're not interrupting anything. Most of my time is alone time," Andrea admitted freely. "I thought you were afraid of storms. What are you doing out here?"

"I am afraid of storms. I just came out to ask you if you wanted to go out for dinner on Sunday?" Heather asked nervously. "To celebrate your birthday," she added to ensure that Andrea knew that she remembered.

Before Andrea could answer, a large bolt of lightning cracked very nearby and Heather jumped into her lap. For several long moments, neither woman moved. They simply gazed into each other's eyes. Heather's hands were resting lightly on Andrea's shoulders. The storm seemed to fade away, and the only thing Heather could see was Andrea.

Heather finally regained her composure and regrettably extricated herself from Andrea's lap.

"Sorry," she said sheepishly, backing away quickly. She was embarrassed by her reaction to the storm and afraid, once again, of her reaction to Andrea.

"No apology necessary," Andrea replied.

Now that Heather was standing a few feet away from her, she was able to consider her response to the question about dinner. She hadn't celebrated her birthday since she was seventeen. Heather had taken her out to dinner that night and then they sat out by the river and talked for hours. It would be nice to spend some time with Heather again, and Dr. Cochran did tell her she needed to discuss things with Heather. It was the only way to move on.

Heather had backtracked so quickly, she had nearly reached the staircase leading back upstairs before Andrea stopped her.

"Heather," Andrea shouted over the sound of the falling rain, "I'd love to go to dinner on Sunday."

Heather was overjoyed. She hoped she didn't have a ridiculous smile on her face as she shouted back, "Good."

Heather ran up the stairs, almost giddy with excitement. She knew exactly what she was going to buy Andie for her birthday. For her sixteenth birthday, she bought her a beautiful gold bracelet. Andrea lost it sometime during the chaos that ensued after her mother's tragic death. It would be the perfect gift. Especially, if she could find one just like it.

Andrea sat for several more minutes until the rain picked up and began falling in sheets. She replayed the last few minutes over again in her mind. What had caused Heather's sudden change of heart? Heather was being nice. She must have some motive for her behaviour. Andrea was also certain that Heather's eyes were full of lust and desire as she sat in her lap.

Must have imagined it, she decided, but she was sure Heather was about to kiss her a second before she got up and moved away.

Chapter 12

When the pilot announced that they were getting ready to begin their decent into Greensboro, Terri suddenly realized that there were a few flaws in her plan. She had decided, after finding out that Andrea's birthday was on Sunday, that she would fly down for the weekend and surprise her. The problem was, she hadn't talked to Andrea all week and had no idea if she'd be alone or even home for that matter. She also didn't know where Andrea's home was. All she had was the address, and she remembered Andrea complaining about how difficult it was to find.

"Excuse me," she said to the beautiful flight attendant who was making her rounds to ensure all the passengers were safely buckled in for landing. "Are you from the Greensboro area?"

"I live about an hour away. Why?"

"I'm flying in to surprise a friend for her birthday and all I have is an address. I haven't the slightest idea where she's staying." As she spoke, she handed the woman, whose nametag read Heather, a piece of paper, which contained the address.

Heather was momentarily speechless as she stared at the piece of paper reading her own address repeatedly, hoping somehow that she was reading it wrong. She selfishly wanted Andie to herself this weekend. She had a decision to make. She could tell this woman the truth and offer her a ride, or she could lie and tell her she didn't know where that was. If she lied, she would likely run into the woman at some point this weekend and that would only increase the tension that existed between herself and Andie.

"Well, this is quite the coincidence, but that's my address. If you can hang around for about a half an hour after the flight, while I finish my reports, I'd be happy to give you a ride," Heather offered.

"You're kidding! Talk about a coincidence!" Terri replied in awe. "Are you sure? I don't want to put you out at all," Terri added sincerely.

"It's really no trouble at all. I'm going right home, so you might as well come along."

"Okay. Thanks. My name is Terri, by the way." Terri couldn't believe her good luck. Maybe this would work out after all. This was more than coincidence; this was fate telling her that her decision to surprise Andrea this weekend was the right one.

"So, Terri, how long have you known Andie?" Heather asked once they were comfortably settled into her car and headed to the house.

"About three years ... She lets you call her Andie?" Terri asked. Terri had called her that once and Andrea freaked out and told her never to call her that again. She never did.

"I've always called her that," Heather said arrogantly, as if this were some sort of competition. "We grew up together," she added, as if to validate her position in Andrea's life.

"Three years is quite a long time," Heather said flatly, as she evaluated the woman riding in the passenger seat. Terri was flawless as far as Heather could tell, and she had no trouble envisioning Terri and Andie together. They would make a stunning couple. Terri's bubbly personality, soft, pretty features, and short blond hair, were a stark contrast to Andie's stoic personality, strong, angular features, and dark hair.

Thinking of the two of them together made Heather sad. She should have known that Andie had a girlfriend. No wonder Andie wasn't interested in her anymore.

"It's funny, Andrea never mentioned you," Terri said thoughtfully.

"I'm not surprised," Heather replied sadly. "We're not that close anymore."

There was something strange in the tone of Heather's voice, Terri thought to herself and then suddenly, the pieces of the puzzle started falling into place. A flash of Andrea's naked body crossed her mind and she zeroed in on the tattoo above Andrea's left hip. It was of the letter H surrounded by a heart. She often wondered about it, but never asked. Assuming the H stood for Heather and they had a history together; and assuming Andrea moved into Heather's house unknowingly; it's no wonder Andrea was behaving strangely since she left for

North Carolina. Whatever was left unresolved between the two of them was having an adverse effect on Andrea.

"We're here," Heather said as they pulled into the long, narrow driveway.

"Nice place," Terri replied honestly. She had lived in the city all her life and only recently, had she moved to a suburb of Cincinnati. She often dreamed about living out in the country but always thought it would be an inconvenience. She liked the fact that she could walk down to the corner store, or call on a neighbour if she needed something. There were definitely no neighbours to call on around here, she noted absentmindedly as she followed Heather up the stairs to the front door.

"Andie doesn't know you're here?" Heather asked before opening the door to step in.

"No. I haven't talked to her since she left on Monday."

This should be interesting, Heather thought to herself. She wondered what Andrea's reaction was going to be at seeing the two of them together.

"Good," she replied to Terri, thinking that she would enjoy watching Andrea squirm, wondering what the two of them had been discussing.

The door swung open and Andrea watched in horror as the two most important women in her life walked through the door together. *This is bad.* She felt the blush creep across her face. She had told neither woman that the other existed. She didn't have to. She wasn't committed to Terri, and Heather wanted nothing to do with her. So why did she feel as if she was hiding something?

"Hi, Ter! What are you doing here?" she asked hesitantly.

"Hey, Reynolds!" Terri replied in greeting before thoroughly kissing her on the lips. Terri felt the tension in Andrea's body grow exponentially as they kissed, thus confirming her earlier assumptions. There was definitely some history between the two women. She wasn't jealous. She just wanted Andrea to be happy.

Terri stood, hands resting lightly on Andrea's chest, looked at her panic-stricken face, and said, "I thought I'd fly down and surprise you for your birthday."

"Well, you definitely succeeded. I don't know that I've ever been more …" she paused. Andrea was going to say; *more surprised to see anyone in my life*, but that wasn't true. Seeing Heather in the kitchen that night was more shocking.

"How did you know?"

"You should be more careful what you leave in people's cars, Reynolds."

At Andrea's puzzled expression, she added, "I found your receipt from the DMV and put two and two together."

"Very clever of you."

"My powers of deduction are greater than you think," Terri said as she looked over at Heather and then back at Andrea.

"Are you going to show me your room?"

"Yes. Sorry. Follow me." She led Terri to her room to put her duffle bag away and left her to freshen up in the bathroom while she went back out to explain things to Heather.

There's nothing to explain, she reminded herself. She had done nothing wrong. She nervously walked into the living room and met Heather's questioning gaze.

"So you met Terri?" she asked hesitantly.

"I did. She's very nice ... and very pretty." Heather hoped that she'd kept her disappointment from showing.

Andrea merely shrugged. She didn't want to agree with Heather's assessment even though it was true.

"I met her on the plane. It was very weird. She asked me for directions, and when I read the address on the piece of paper she was showing me, well, imagine my surprise, when I saw it was my own," Heather said.

Andrea looked at her in disbelief. Why was this happening now? Things were just starting to look up between her and Heather and now Terri was here. Not that she wasn't happy to see Terri. It was very thoughtful of her to fly down to surprise her, but she was hoping that she'd be able to spend some time with Heather this weekend.

"It was very nice of you to offer her a ride."

Before Heather could reply, Terri returned and wrapped her arms around Andrea's waist possessively.

"Baby, I'm starving," Terri said.

"Me too." She lied. Her appetite was long gone, but the thought of getting Terri out of the house, and away from Heather, was appealing.

"Give me a couple of minutes to shower and then I'll take you out. You can wait in my room."

"I think I'll wait right here, if that's okay?"

"Okay. I'll be quick," Andrea replied as she turned and walked away.

This is bad ... so very bad, she mumbled under her breath as she entered her bedroom.

Heather saw Terri roll her eyes when Andrea mentioned taking a shower. She had a suspicion that maybe Andrea hadn't told her about her past.

"I see she still has that obsessive compulsive shower thing," Heather said.

"Oh, yeah," Terri replied dejectedly.

"Has she told you why?" Heather asked, wanting to gauge the closeness of their relationship.

"No. I just figured it was some weird compulsion."

"Well, it is. But there's a reason for it," Heather said.

At Terri's questioning look, Heather continued, "It started the night her mother was attacked. When she got to my house, after leaving the hospital, her clothes were covered in blood. Ever since then, she's been trying to wash away the blood and the guilt."

Terri didn't know what to say. She felt bad for feeling annoyed in the past.

"I didn't know. She never really talks about it."

"She never did talk about it. I knew the details of course, being so close to the situation, but she just sort of shut down after it happened. She wouldn't talk about it," Heather said sympathetically.

Heather took Terri on a brief tour of the house before rejoining a nervous looking Andrea in the living room a few minutes later.

"Ready to go?" Andrea asked, eager to get Terri away from Heather. Andrea extended her arm and curled it around Terri's waist as she urged her toward the door.

Once in the car and headed toward the restaurant, Terri asked, "Why have you never mentioned Heather before?"

"Why would I have?" Andrea replied innocently.

Terri took a moment to contemplate Andrea's answer. She could push the issue and probably end up arguing all night, or she could let it go for now, and enjoy a wonderful evening with Andrea, which is why she flew down in the first place.

"I guess you wouldn't have. Do you have any plans for tomorrow?" she asked, decidedly changing the subject.

"No. Just another day," Andrea replied, despite her dinner plans with Heather tomorrow night.

"It's sad that you have no plans for your birthday, but I'm glad you don't. I was worried I was making this trip for nothing."

"When is your flight back?"

"Tomorrow at five."

Andrea was slightly relieved. There would still be time to go to dinner with Heather, if she was still willing, after Terri was gone.

Chapter 13

The previous night had been long and Andrea was still sound asleep when Terri quietly crawled out of bed and made her way to the kitchen. Andrea had taken her to a fabulous Mexican restaurant, where they lingered for quite some time after dinner over shared deep fried ice cream and virgin margaritas. Andrea suggested they stop by a club afterward so that they could dance for a little while and say hi to some of her friends.

They were still at the club for last call and Terri wondered if Andrea had been avoiding going home for some reason. They had a wonderful time, regardless of Andrea's motives, and Terri was grateful to have met Tammy, whom she immediately thought of as her friend.

By the time they arrived home, around three in the morning, Terri was exhausted, and Andrea didn't seem the least bit interested in making love. She wondered if Andrea's lack of interest was a result of fatigue or the fact that Heather was in the room next to them.

Terri was happily preparing pancakes for breakfast when Heather walked into the kitchen.

"Good morning," she said to the sleepy-eyed woman.

Heather stared at her for the longest time. Terri was wearing one of Andie's shirts and the sight brought a flood of memories rushing back to her. How many times had Heather hidden one of Andie's t-shirts and worn it to school under her sweatshirt? The comfort she felt from the lingering and intoxicating scent that was Andie stayed with her all day.

"Morning," she replied. Heather wanted to dislike this woman, but she couldn't. There was nothing to dislike.

"You know, if you throw some chocolate chips in those, Andie will love you forever." As the words were leaving her mouth, Heather regretted saying them. Why was she telling this woman how to make Andie happy?

"Really?" Terri questioned as she found some chocolate chips and added them to the batter.

"May I ask you a question?" Terri said.

"Sure," Heather replied hesitantly. She was worried about what Terri might ask. She seemed like the kind of person who wouldn't pull any punches.

"Are you in love with Andrea?" Terri's voice was calm and cool. There was no accusation in her voice.

Heather panicked. Her hands began to shake. Beads of sweat formed on her forehead. "God no!" She attempted to sound appalled at the question. "Why would you ask me that?" she replied defensively.

"I don't know. It's just that you seem so different when she's around. Your face lights up. Your breathing changes …"

Heather interrupted her. "Whatever you think you're seeing, you must be imagining. I'm not in love with Andie." How could Andie be so clueless about the depths of Heather's feelings for her and yet, Terri, a perfect stranger, noticed them immediately?

"I'm sorry if I upset you. I just had to ask," Terri replied before leaving the room, plates of pancakes in hand. She could see right through Heather's lie and wondered what had happened between these two women who seemed to love each other so much.

Andrea had rolled over to Terri's side of the bed and was hugging her pillow. She looked so vulnerable and peaceful lying there, that Terri thought twice before waking her.

"Hey, baby," she whispered gently as she brushed the hair from Andrea's forehead with her fingers.

Andrea opened her eyes and suddenly remembered the predicament she was in.

"Good morning, Ter." This was going to be a long day. She needed to find a way to keep Terri and Heather apart.

"Happy birthday!" Terri said as she handed Andrea her plate.

"Are those chocolate chips?" she asked excitedly.

"Yup! A little birdie told me that you liked chocolate chip pancakes. How come you never told me?"

Andrea couldn't believe that Heather remembered such a minute detail about her or that she had told Terri about it.

"I thought you would think it was childish of me, so I never said anything."

Terri shook her head and smiled as she retrieved an envelope from her duffle bag.

"Here's your gift. I hope you like it."

Andrea took the offered envelope and looked at it for several long minutes. She hadn't received a birthday gift in years. It felt strange. She didn't know how to respond.

When Andrea didn't make a move to open it, Terri offered her some encouragement. "Open it already, Reynolds. We haven't got all day."

Andrea finally slid the envelope open and gasped when she saw the contents. Inside were two tickets to the Carolina Panthers game in a couple of weeks. Upon closer examination, she noticed that the seats were in the eighth row near the fifty-yard line.

"Terri, I don't know what to say. These are great. How did you ..." She stopped herself before she could finish asking how Terri got the tickets. The same way she got the car and the house.

"Thank you." She kissed Terri softly on the lips.

"I wasn't sure of your schedule, so I didn't know if you'd be able to make it home for a Bengal's game. I figured you'd at least be able to get away for a Panther's game. I'm sure you can find someone to go with you," Terri said.

"You can't come?" Andrea asked with a hint of disappointment.

"No. I have plans that weekend, and you know I don't like football."

"I wish you could come, but I'm sure I can find someone to go with me."

"I think you should ask Heather," Terri said flatly.

"Why Heather?"

"Are you blind, Reynolds, or just plain stupid?" She paused momentarily to consider the magnitude of what she was about to do.

"That woman is in love with you, and I don't know what stupid thing you did to put that hurt in her eyes, but you better find a way to make up for it." She let out a frustrated breath.

"You have no idea what you're talking about," Andrea replied angrily. Heather wasn't in love with her. How could she be? As far as she knew, Heather still hated her. It wasn't any of Terri's business anyhow.

"Trust me, Reynolds." She took Andrea's hands in hers and looked her square in the eyes. "It doesn't take a genius to look at the two of you and realize that you're in love with each other. The only question is what did you do to hurt her, and can you fix it?"

Andrea sat silently for several long seconds. She was in shock. The only thing she was sure of was that she was in love with Heather. Always had been ... always would be. If Terri was right, maybe there was a chance that she and Heather could be together. Since seeing Heather again, the thought of the two of them together crossed her mind frequently, but when it did, she quickly chased the notion away. It was easier not to get her hopes up. Even when Heather invited her to dinner, she tried not to allow her heart to make it more than it was. It was just dinner. Heather was just being friendly. Maybe Heather felt sorry for her.

"What did you do, Reynolds? Did you cheat on her or something?" Terri asked.

Terri wanted to know what grave injustice Andrea had committed. It had to be something serious to keep the two of them apart when it seemed like they belonged together more than any two people she had ever known.

"No, it wasn't like that," Andrea replied.

Andrea toyed with the idea of telling Terri a lie. It would be easier than telling her the truth, but she owed her the truth, didn't she? Terri was the only constant in her life. Her safe person. The person who accepted her as she was and never asked anything of her. Yes, she owed Terri the truth.

Andrea told Terri the entire story in agonizing detail and then waited for one of her witty remarks about how stupid she was. When it didn't come, she looked at Terri questioningly and said, "Well?"

"Well, it doesn't sound like it was one of your better moments, but don't you think she bears some of the responsibility? I mean, lord knows you're oblivious to the things going on around you. I practically had to throw myself at you to get you to ask me out." She smiled sympathetically. "I just think she should have told you how she felt."

"You sound like my therapist. She thinks I blame Heather for making me do what I did. The thing is, I don't know what Heather was feeling back then. As far as I knew, she was straight. It wasn't until I found out about her and Rebecca that I even considered she might have had feelings for me." Andrea sighed and covered her face with her hands.

"I was just so young and so scared. I wouldn't have survived if she had rejected me."

Terri pulled Andrea's hands away from her face and looked at her tenderly.

"You're not so young anymore, Reynolds, and from what I can tell, you have nothing to lose this time, so get yourself together and figure out a way to make her forgive you."

Heather sat anxiously in the living room, staring blankly at the television. It wasn't even turned on. Her thoughts were fixated on what was potentially going on in Andrea's bedroom. She listened intently but couldn't hear any sounds. She wasn't sure if that was a good thing or a bad thing.

And the nerve of Terri to ask her if she was in love with Andrea. Of course she was. She always would be, but that was none of Terri's business. Instead of offering her a ride home, she should have just jumped on the next plane to anywhere. It would have been a lot less confusing and a lot less painful.

She wished Rebecca was home to help distract her but she was gone away for the weekend to visit her parents. She had to do something. She couldn't just sit there like that, letting her mind create all kinds of unsettling images for her. She picked up the phone and dialed the familiar number.

"Hi, Mom!" she said in her best fake-happy voice when her mother answered the phone.

"What's wrong, sweetheart?" her mother asked knowingly, not at all fooled by Heather's cheery greeting.

"Nothing's wrong, Mom. I was just sitting here wondering what your plans were for Thanksgiving. How would you and daddy feel about flying up here for the weekend?"

"That sounds like a fantastic idea, Heather, but I know that's not the reason for your call. Tell me what's bothering you."

"Do you know what today is?" Heather asked with a hint of challenge in her voice.

Mrs. Johnson glanced over at the calendar on the wall. *Shit*, she thought to herself.

"Of course I do. It's Andrea's birthday. I'm sorry, sweetheart. I didn't realize it until just now. No wonder you sound so sad."

"Mom, I need to tell you something ... Andie's been living here for the last two months." Heather took a deep breath and waited for her mother's reply.

There was nothing but silence on the other end of the line.

"Mom?"

"You don't seem happy about that, Heather," was her mother's reply.

Heather told her mother the entire saga from the night she first saw Andie in the kitchen and wanted to ask her to move out, right up to what happened yesterday with Terri. She managed to hold back the tears until she was through, but now they flowed freely as her mother tried to console her.

"Heather, what is it you want from Andrea?" her mother asked.

"Want?" Heather asked between sobs. "I want her to love me."

"Why? Do you want her to love you because you want to be with her, or do you want her to love you so you can reject her … maybe to get even with her?"

Heather was appalled. How could her own mother ask her a question like that? Why was she so obsessed with wanting Andie to love her? Could her mother be right?

"I don't know, Mom. I have to go."

"Okay, Heather. Just think about what I said. I love you."

"Love you too, Mom."

Heather sat dumbfounded, staring at the phone in her hand after she hung up. She had never considered the possibility that her need for Andie to love her was just a way for her to get even. If Andie loved her, would she reject her—use the power she held to get even with Andie for hurting her. Could she be that cold and calculating?

Heather thought about the jealousy she felt, first when Tammy came to visit, then when Andie went home for the weekend, and now with Terri. If this was just revenge, she wouldn't feel that jealousy, would she? Physical attraction aside, she was still attracted to Andie's stoic personality. She had always been enthralled with Andie's quiet outer strength, and her soft, gentle core. It had taken her years to get to a point where she thought she had figured Andie out, and it wasn't until the day she left, that she realized she hadn't even begun to understand her. The woman was still an unsolved mystery, and Heather wanted to be the one to solve it.

No, this wasn't about revenge; it was about love. She was in love with Andie, but even if Andie one day reciprocated those feelings, would she be able to forgive her, and accept that love? If she couldn't, they would be destined to fail. Regardless of Andie's feelings toward her, Heather knew that she had to find a way to forgive her before anything else could develop. How could she forgive her if she didn't understand why she did it? It was *what* she did that hurt her, but maybe the why would help her understand.

Terri emerged from the bedroom to find Heather sitting on the couch, staring off into space. She could tell she had been crying.

"Hey, are you okay?" Terri asked sincerely.

"Yeah, I'm fine. Just emotional today … must be PMS or something." Heather quickly wiped the tears from her face with her shirtsleeve and tried to look composed as she regarded Terri curiously. She wondered what went on in that bedroom during the last four hours and tried to find a way to hate this woman. For some reason, she just couldn't.

"Andrea tells me that you're taking her out to dinner tonight."

"I was," Heather replied dejectedly.

"You mean you're not taking her now?" Terri asked, slightly annoyed at Heather's passiveness. Terri thought that Heather should be fighting for Andrea; protecting her territory—especially since she had arrived and wrecked her plans. Instead, it seemed that Heather had simply accepted defeat. Between the two of them, dancing around their feelings the way they were, it was no wonder that they weren't together.

"I just figured she'd want to be with you, especially since you came all this way to surprise her," Heather said.

"What is it with you two?" Terri was frustrated. "I'm leaving in a couple of hours. This is what's going to happen ... you are going to come with us to the airport and then, you are going to take her out to dinner like you planned ... and for Christ's sake, talk to each other!" Terri was so frustrated by this point that she didn't wait for a response. She headed directly to the bedroom and joined Andrea in the shower.

Andrea immediately tensed up when Terri took the soapy washcloth from her hand and began washing her back.

"Relax, Reynolds, I'm just going to wash your back," Terri said.

"It's just that ..."

"I know, baby. Don't worry. I understand," Terri replied sympathetically and kissed Andrea lightly on the shoulder.

"I think you should wear your new jeans to dinner, and the shirt I bought you. You look so sexy in it."

"What are you talking about?" Andrea asked.

"Your dinner with Heather tonight. You'll be nearly irresistible."

"She probably won't want to go now," Andrea replied dejectedly.

"I sort of told her she didn't have a choice. If the two of you have a chance in hell, tonight has to go well. You have to talk to each other. I swear I'm dealing with a couple of children," Terri said assertively.

"You told her she *had* to take me to dinner. That's great! Now I won't know if she's just doing it because she feels like she has to, or because she wants to."

"She wants to. Trust me. If I wasn't so sure about this, do you think I'd be letting you go so easily? You know how much I enjoy your company. If I didn't know you were meant for each other, I'd be fighting to keep you for myself."

Terri turned Andrea around so she could look in her eyes.

"Trust me," she said one final time before kissing Andrea on the cheek, stepping out of the shower, and wrapping herself in Andrea's robe.

"You must be the most unselfish person I've ever met, Ter," Andrea said through the shower door.

"Don't you ever forget it, Reynolds," Terri replied with a laugh and handed Andrea an oversized bath towel.

Heather was standing in her bedroom wrapped in a towel, looking for something to wear to dinner. She was upset with Terri for interfering, but at the same time, she was excited that her plans with Andie weren't cancelled after all. What did Terri mean by they had to talk to each other? What went on between her and Andie was none of Terri's business—or was it? Being Andie's girlfriend entitled Terri to interfere in certain aspects of her life, right?

What was she going to wear? Would Terri get jealous and tell Andrea she couldn't have dinner with Heather if she was dressed too sexily? It was all too much to think about. As if the stress of going to dinner alone with Andie wasn't enough; now, she had to deal with all these other technicalities.

Since it was unusually warm for this time of year, Heather decided to wear a sexy low-cut tank top and cover it with a light sweater that she could either unbutton or remove altogether after they dropped Terri off at the airport.

Chapter 14

▼

I'm alone with Heather, I'm alone with Heather, Andrea's happy voice was saying in her head as they pulled out of the airport and onto the highway. Suddenly, her happy voice turned into a voice of terror, *I'm alone with Heather, what do I do?*

Andrea had mixed feelings. Terri kissed her softly on the lips before getting out of the car at the airport and said, "I'll miss you, Reynolds. If things don't work out, you know where to find me."

She would miss Terri's adventurous and playful attitude. It's not to say that Andrea had been inexperienced when she met Terri, but who knew the fun you could have with a package of Pop Rocks, a Popsicle, and hot candle wax on a rainy Sunday afternoon? Terri did—that's who. Yes, Andrea would definitely miss Terri. She was sad about that, but on the other hand, she was about to embark on an entirely different journey with the woman she loved more than anything in the world. She was excited and terrified about that.

She glanced over at Heather, who was sitting quietly in the passenger seat looking out the window, apparently deep in thought. The silence was uncomfortable. She wanted to say something, but couldn't come up with anything to say. If Heather was as uncomfortable as she was, maybe this wasn't such a good idea. She decided to give her the chance to opt out if she wanted to.

"Heather, if you'd rather just go home, I'll understand."

"Is that what you want?"

Time for a little honesty.

"No, that's not what I want. I've been looking forward to this since you asked me," Andrea admitted.

Heather looked at her and smiled. "Good. Me too."

Andrea smiled back, relieved that Heather seemed as excited as she was. The uncomfortable feeling was fading until Heather decided to bring up Terri again.

"You and Terri have been seeing each other for a few years. That's quite a long time." It was said as more of a question than a statement, leaving Andrea no choice but to answer.

"Yeah, but it's not serious, if that's what you think."

"How can it not be serious?" Heather questioned.

"I don't know, Heather. I can't really explain it. It just isn't."

"Okay, don't get all defensive about it. It was just a question."

Andrea pulled into a parking space near the entrance to the restaurant and looked over to Heather.

"I'm sorry. It's just that Terri and I decided not to see each other anymore ... can we not talk about her, I'm starving." She opened the car door and started to step out but Heather grabbed her arm and pulled her back into the car.

"Wait. She broke up with you on your birthday?" Heather was appalled. How could someone be so cold?

"She didn't break up with me, we weren't really a couple. We both dated other people. That's just the way it was and we both decided that maybe it would be best to give it a rest for a little while," Andrea insisted.

Heather's mood suddenly shifted. Instantly, the dark cloud that had been looming over her since finding out about Terri lifted and she felt a glimmer of hope. Maybe Andrea was available after all. The gloomy feeling returned without warning. If Andrea wasn't seeing anyone, then why hadn't she shown any interest in her? This emotional roller coaster was making her nauseous.

Andrea watched Heather's expression change from sad, to happy, to angry, and wondered what she had said to cause it. She decided that trying to figure out what Heather was thinking was almost impossible.

"Can we go in now?" Andrea asked.

"Okay," Heather replied and walked with Andrea through the door where an overly friendly hostess, who seemed to feel the need to touch Andie while she talked, ushered them to a table in the far corner of the restaurant.

The hostess was smiling dreamily into Andie's eyes as she handed them each a menu and told them that their server would be over shortly to take their drink orders.

"What?" Andrea asked in response to Heather's disapproving glare.

"She could have been a little more subtle, don't you think? What if this had been an actual date? I should go over there and tell her to keep her hands, and her eyes, to herself."

Heather understood why the woman was fawning all over Andie, it was impossible not to. She looked so good in that shirt, that Heather found herself having to avoid looking at her while she was talking to her; otherwise, she lost all train of thought.

"I thought she was just being friendly," Andrea replied innocently.

"You really are dense sometimes, Andie."

"That's funny. That's the second time I've been told that today."

Just then, their server arrived to take their drink orders. Andrea thought about ordering something to help calm her nerves but remembered her promise to Tammy and ordered a Coke instead.

They perused the menu in silence while they waited for their drinks to arrive. Andie was having a difficult time focussing on her menu with Heather sitting across from her, especially now that she had unbuttoned her sweater. Andie's eyes kept peering over her menu at the hint of bronzed cleavage that was taunting her. She still hadn't fully recovered from seeing Heather naked the other day.

Heather was pleased that unbuttoning her sweater was having the desired effect. Andie was finally showing some interest. She thought about removing the sweater completely, but the chill of the air conditioner was more than she could handle, so she left it on.

After the server had taken their orders and left the table, they started talking mindlessly about their jobs, the weather, and anything else that wouldn't evoke any emotion. They were both treading carefully, trying to avoid saying anything that might upset the other. The tension was building. The things that were going unsaid between them were bubbling like a pot left on a stove. Eventually, it was going to boil over and it was going to be messy. Luckily, their meals arrived before the boiling point and the unsaid things were left simmering on a back burner while they ate.

Heather playfully stabbed a piece of steak off of Andrea's plate and laughed at Andrea's phoney appalled expression. That's the way things used to be between the two of them, and Heather wanted so badly to let go of the hurt so that things could be that way again. She couldn't just let it go though. She had to know why, but she didn't want to spoil this wonderful moment.

"Can I get you ladies anything else?" the server asked while she cleared their dinner plates.

"Since my friend here ate most of my steak, I'm still hungry and would like to see a dessert menu please," Andrea said to the server, who smiled at her and handed her the requested menu.

"I'll get rid of these plates and be right back to take your order."

"I only had a few bites," Heather protested.

"I know. I was only teasing. I'm actually not all that hungry, how 'bout we share?" Andrea suggested.

"Okay. It's your birthday though, so you choose."

When the server returned, Andrea ordered the Triple Chocolate Pecan Cheesecake with two forks.

"You know, Andie, I never thanked you for the watch. I love it. It's the one I'd been saving up to buy."

"When I saw it, I knew I had to get it for you. I'm glad you like it. I was worried ..."

"Here you go ladies, enjoy," the server interrupted.

Andrea took a forkful of the delicious looking dessert and held it up in offering to Heather. Just as Heather opened her mouth to accept it, Andrea pulled her arm back and put the fork in her own mouth.

"Mmmm!" Andrea smiled as she exaggerated her appreciation for the wonderful flavour.

"What?" Andrea asked in response to Heather's evil glare.

"You're mean," Heather pouted.

"Am I? I figured, since it was my birthday, I should have the first bite." She quickly gathered another bite on her fork and held it out to Heather.

"Here."

Just as Heather was about to close her mouth over the fork, Andrea once again stole the bite for herself and laughed.

"It's really good, Heather. You should try some," Andrea teased and grabbed another forkful and once again offered it to Heather.

This time Heather grabbed Andrea's wrist before she had a chance to pull it away. She licked her lips seductively while looking into Andrea's eyes and slowly, teasingly closed her lips over the fork, savouring the flavour and the effect her little display was having on Andie.

Andrea's mouth fell open as she struggled to draw breath. She could see her hand shaking but was powerless to stop it. Her heart was beating so hard against her chest that it was almost painful. Just then, the server returned with their bill and Heather released her grip on Andie's arm.

There goes half of your tip, Heather thought to herself, angry that the woman decided to pick that very moment to interrupt them. She handed the woman a credit card, picked the second fork up off the table, and quietly helped Andie finish the dessert.

As they exited the restaurant, Andrea caught Heather glaring at the hostess. *Was that jealousy?* Andrea found it amusing. Maybe Terri was right.

Andrea started the car and decided that she wasn't ready to put an end to the wonderful evening they had been having. It was the first step in making things right between them, but they still hadn't talked about anything important. She knew they had to go back, if they were ever going to go forward.

"Thanks for dinner, Heather. It was great," Andrea said sincerely. She paused nervously before continuing. "Are you in a hurry to get home, or do you want to go for a walk or something?"

Heather did not want to ruin this evening with an argument, but saw Andie's invitation to go for a walk, as an invitation to talk. She may not get another chance.

"Sure. There's a park down the road. Why don't we go there and walk around?" Heather suggested.

Andrea followed Heather's directions intently, all the while growing increasingly anxious. She had the unsettling feeling that the conversation they were going to have during this walk was not going to be as pleasant as the one during dinner.

When they arrived at the park, Heather pulled a small box out of the backseat and handed it to Andrea. She knew Andie was uncomfortable accepting gifts so she decided to give her the option of opening it later on her own.

"You can open it later if you want."

"You didn't have to do this, Heather. Dinner was more than enough," Andrea said as she stared at the small box in her hand, trying to decide if she should open it or not.

"I know, I didn't have to, I wanted to." She fought the urge to touch Andie's arm as she spoke.

After a few minutes of silence, Andrea carefully opened the box.

"Heather ... I ... How did ... It's exactly like the one I lost," she finally managed to say as she fought back the tears.

"Not exactly. I didn't get a chance to get it engraved, but otherwise, yes, it's the same."

"I don't know what to say, Heather. Thank you, it's beautiful." She removed it from the box and struggled with the clasp while trying to put it on her wrist.

"Here, let me help you."

Andrea's skin tingled where Heather's fingertips touched her. Controlling her body's reaction to Heather was growing increasingly difficult. She wondered if Heather could tell.

"Well, are we going to go for a walk or are we going to sit here and stare at your wrist all day?" Heather asked.

Andrea took a deep breath and exited the car knowing that when they returned, things between them would be different. The only question was, would they be better or worse.

They walked along in silence, neither woman wanting to be the one to break the harmony until finally, Heather gathered enough courage to speak.

"I know we're having a good time, and I don't want to ruin that by bringing up old dirt, but I have to ask you something."

"Ask," Andrea said bravely, even though she was terrified of what that question was going to be.

"Why?" Heather asked, knowing that she didn't have to elaborate.

"I could ask you the same question," Andrea shot back.

"What is that supposed to mean?"

"It means, why didn't you tell me, or give me some kind of clue, or something?"

"I gave you plenty of clues, it's not my fault you didn't see them," Heather accused.

"Sure, now that I look back on it, there were clues … You were at all my games, even my practices … you never dated anyone—except for that one guy, Matt … and you paraded around naked all the time. That was a particularly trying year. Why'd you stop by the way?" Andrea asked.

"I stopped because it killed me that you didn't react," Heather admitted.

"I reacted all right. I just didn't let you see it. Those were the nights I slept in the chair, afraid that if I slept in the bed with you, I might do something we'd both regret."

"I wouldn't have regretted it. Matt meant nothing, by the way. On our third date, he tried to kiss me and I bit his lip." Heather chuckled at the memory.

"Why didn't you tell me?"

"I was so upset and grossed out by it, I went looking for you afterwards, but you weren't home, and you never asked me about it, so I figured you didn't care," Heather replied.

"I did care. I was so jealous. I couldn't handle you talking about dating some guy. It drove me crazy. That's why I stayed away from you. After school, I'd just go hang out by the river until I knew it was past your curfew."

"You haven't answered my original question," Heather said.

Andrea let out a frustrated sigh. "About two weeks before we were going to leave for college, I almost kissed you. It wasn't the first time. It was getting harder and harder to hide my feelings, and I knew I wouldn't have survived if you rejected me." Andrea stopped walking and turned to face Heather.

"I honestly thought I was doing the right thing. I thought it would only be me who would suffer for my decision. As far as I knew, you were straight. I figured that you'd be angry or grossed out by the kiss and be happy to have me out of your life. I never once thought that you were feeling the same way."

Heather didn't know what she expected Andie's response to be, but that wasn't it. How could she stay angry with her after hearing the truth?

"All this time, I thought you had rejected me, or that I was a lousy kisser. I guess I never realized the sacrifice that you were making by leaving. That was the happiest and saddest day of my life," Heather said truthfully.

"I'm sorry, Heather. I would do things differently if I could do them over again," Andrea said regretfully.

"Me too," Heather replied softly. "I would have attacked you in your sleep." She laughed mischievously and started to run through the park so that Andrea would have to run after her.

For a long time Andrea just toyed with her. She knew she could run faster than Heather, but she was enjoying this little game. She would run fast and almost catch her, then slow way down to let Heather gain some distance on her.

It was starting to get dark, so Andrea hid behind a tree and watched for a long time as Heather searched for her. If she got close, Andrea would move to the other side of the tree. It was almost too easy. Once it appeared Heather was giving up, Andrea snuck up on her and scared her. What she hadn't planned on, was that Heather would be so scared she'd freak out and start punching her.

In her haste to get out of Heather's reach, Andrea tripped and landed flat out on her back, pulling Heather down with her.

"Are you okay?" the panicked Heather asked.

Andrea faked unconsciousness.

"Andie? Wake up. Oh my God! Andie?" Heather was shouting and slapping Andrea's face trying to get her to wake up. Finally, Andrea could take no more and busted out laughing which caused Heather to start hitting her again.

"I hate you. That wasn't funny. Why did you do that?"

Andrea kept laughing and Heather kept punching her.

"Ouch!" Andrea shouted. She wasn't hurt, but it caused enough of a distraction for Heather to stop punching her. Andrea grabbed her wrists and rolled them over so she was lying on top.

Suddenly, the game was over. They weren't laughing anymore. They were both breathing heavily. For the first time in her life, Heather saw something in

Andie's eyes. There was a hunger there that she had never seen before. She knew Andie was going to kiss her. She took a deep breath and stared at Andie's lips, as they got closer and closer to hers.

"Heather, I ..." A bright light shinning in Andrea's eyes caused her to look up.

"Hey! Are you two okay over there?" asked the security guard with the flashlight who was patrolling the park.

Andrea stood up quickly.

"We're fine," she shouted, and pulled Heather up off the ground. They quickly walked back to the car giggling like a couple of schoolgirls.

When they got home, Andrea pulled Heather into a hug, and kissed her on the cheek. "Thanks Heather. I can't remember the last time I had so much fun."

"Maybe we could do it again sometime," Heather suggested once they reached the living room. She was standing there hoping that Andie would finish what she started in the park, but when she made a move toward her bedroom, she knew the moment was lost forever.

"Actually, are you working the Sunday after next?" Andrea asked shyly.

"No. Why?"

"Would you like to go to a football game with me?"

"I'd love to," Heather replied, despite the fact that she hated football.

"Great. Thanks again for tonight. Goodnight."

"Goodnight, Andie."

Andrea sat on the edge of her bed for a long time, replaying the events of the evening. She couldn't believe how close she had come to kissing Heather again. It just seemed as though there was some evil spirit working against her, interfering at the most inopportune time. She stared down at the bracelet on her wrist with a newfound hope that maybe she did have a chance to start all over again with Heather.

Chapter 15

Heather rolled over and sighed audibly at the sight of Rebecca sleeping peacefully beside her. Since her dinner with Andie a couple of weeks ago, she had little interest in Rebecca anymore. Even though there was nothing going on between her and Andie, she didn't feel right making love to Rebecca. When Rebecca tried to initiate sex, Heather came up with excuses. She'd say she was too tired or she wasn't feeling well. Sometimes she'd pretend to be sleeping. She had given in once, though her participation was limited and half-hearted. She felt inexplicably guilty afterward.

She rolled back over, faced the wall, and thought about what her day with Andie would be like. Although they hadn't seen much of each other the last two weeks, the tension that existed between them over what happened eight years ago was gone. Something worse existed between them now—sexual tension. They both knew it, both felt it, but neither of them was willing to take the risk. Maybe it was better just to leave things as they were.

Andrea got out of bed and stretched languidly. She'd been up for hours, unable to sleep because of her excitement over spending the day with Heather. She wondered if Heather was in love with Rebecca. They seemed like a happy couple, even though she couldn't understand their relationship. She thought they just didn't suit each other. She promised herself, after her near slip up in the park, that she wouldn't pursue Heather while she was with Rebecca. It wasn't fair to Rebecca. If Heather wanted to be with her, instead of Rebecca, then she would have to end their relationship.

She showered, got dressed, and joined Heather and Rebecca in the living room.

"Morning, Andie," Heather said with more enthusiasm than she should have.

"Hi," Andrea replied nervously in response to the scrutinizing glare she was receiving from Rebecca.

"I can't believe you invited Heather to the game," Rebecca said almost angrily.

"Why?" Andrea asked, even though she was sure Rebecca was jealous. What she couldn't figure out was, was she jealous that Heather was going with *her*, or just that Heather was going.

"Heather doesn't even like football," Rebecca whined.

"She doesn't?" Andrea questioned and looked over at Heather for confirmation.

Heather looked like a deer caught in someone's headlights. She didn't know what to do. No, she didn't like football, but she would have done anything if it meant spending the day with Andie.

"I like football," she said as convincingly as possible.

"Then how come you never watch it with me on TV, or when I ask you if you want to go to a game, you say you'd rather not?" Rebecca questioned.

"I don't know. Maybe you just asked at the wrong time." Heather was desperately trying to dig her way out of this mess.

"Whatever ... I just can't imagine Andrea wasting a perfectly good ticket on someone who doesn't enjoy the game." Rebecca stood up and left the room in protest.

"Sorry. If I had known it was going to cause such a problem, I wouldn't have asked you," Andrea said sympathetically.

"She'll get over it," Heather assured.

"You really don't like football, do you?"

"No, not really," Heather admitted.

"Then why did you agree to go? And why did you go to all those games with me back home?"

"You really are dense, aren't you Andie?" Heather smiled and made her way to the kitchen to prepare breakfast.

"I'm sorry I didn't plan better," Andrea said when they finally found a parking space, five blocks away from the stadium. "If we hurry, we might just make it to our seats before kick-off."

"You know, I don't care if I see any of the game," Heather admitted as she tried to keep pace with the nearly jogging Andrea.

Andrea smiled and slowed her pace slightly to allow Heather to catch up. When they made their way into the stadium, the concourse area was swarming with people, eagerly trying to find their seats. She was concerned that she might lose track of Heather in the giant mass of bodies. Without thinking, she reached out and took Heather's hand in hers.

The innocent contact of Heather's small warm hand in hers sent a surge of excitement through her body and she no longer cared if she saw any of the game either. As they approached their section, she secretly considered walking past it, in order to prolong the contact, but decided against it, and ushered Heather to their seats just in time to see the kick-off.

"Which team are we rooting for?" Heather asked.

"The blue team," Andrea explained. "The Panthers. They will probably lose, because they're playing the Colts, but they're the home team, so that's who we root for."

"Okay," Heather replied and tried to make herself comfortable in her seat. There was a big burly man sitting to her right, who was invading her personal space.

Andrea stretched in her seat and her knee inadvertently came to rest against Heather's. She thought about quickly moving her leg, but when Heather shifted in her seat to enhance the contact, she let out the breath she'd been holding and relaxed.

When the Panther's marched down the field after the opening kick-off, to score a touchdown, everyone in the stadium roared to life. Everyone expected the Colts to annihilate the Panthers, so when the Panthers took the early lead, there was a cautious optimism floating through the crowd.

Reality set in late in the second quarter when it appeared the Colts finally realized they were playing in this game, not just watching it. They went to the locker room at half-time leading 10-7.

"Are you hungry?" Andrea asked when Heather stood up to stretch her legs and get away from the big burly man for a few minutes.

"Yeah, a little bit. I'm craving a hotdog. It's been years since I've had one."

"Then, a hotdog, you shall have. Do you want to come with me or just stay here?" Andrea asked.

Heather looked up at the sea of people swarming around, pushing and shoving to get to their destination, and decided to stay where she was.

"Do you mind if I stay here?" she asked innocently.

"I'd actually prefer it; I'd probably lose you up there. Just mustard, right?"

"I'm surprised you remembered," Heather replied truthfully.

"I remember everything about you," Andrea admitted as she walked away, afraid to witness Heather's response to that statement.

Andrea ducked, swerved, and slinked her way through the crowd and to the souvenir booth. While she was sitting next to Heather, she realized that her eyes were nearly the same colour as the Panther's jerseys. She bought the smallest adult shirt possible, thinking that it still seemed too big for Heather's tiny frame, and made her way to the food vendors.

By the time she returned to her seat, she had missed the second half kick-off, but the smile on Heather's face instantly dissolved her disappointment. She handed Heather her food and took her seat.

"You've got some mustard here," Andrea said as she indicated its location on her own face.

After several failed attempts at removing the offending yellow substance from her face, Andrea laughed at her. Heather just kept missing it.

"Here, I'll get it," Andrea finally said, unable to watch Heather's frustrated attempts any longer.

Andrea reached over to swipe the smudge away with her thumb, but with Heather's eyes fixated on hers and the unbelievably soft skin of her face pressed against her palm, she froze in place. The crowd around them faded away and all Andrea could see was Heather's beautiful face. She wanted so badly to kiss her, and might just have, had the crowd not come to life and roared suddenly at some magnificent play on the field.

Jarred back into reality, Andrea wiped the mustard away and returned her attention to the game. Midway through the fourth quarter, the Colts had such a substantial lead that the fans started to make their way out of the stadium in droves.

"Do you want to leave?" Andrea asked.

"Not really," Heather admitted. She wanted this game to last as long as possible. Despite the fact that she had no idea who was winning or losing or what the score even was, she was having a wonderful time just being with Andie. She would gladly sit through a root canal if Andie were sitting there with her.

"I almost forgot," Andrea said as she reached for the bag she had placed under her seat.

"I bought this for you. I know it's not something you would wear very often, but the blue matches your eyes and there's something a little bit sexy about a girl wearing a football jersey." Andrea felt the crimson blush creep across her face. *I didn't just say that out loud, did I?*

"Is that just your opinion, or do a lot of people find girls in football jerseys sexy?" Heather asked with a chuckle. She found Andrea's embarrassment adorable.

Andrea didn't answer the question. She covered her eyes with her hands and couldn't look at Heather again until she said, "What do you think, Andie? Do I look sexy?"

Andrea looked over at Heather's tiny body swimming in the oversize jersey. Her breath caught. Speaking was not an option. Arousal shot through her body like a bolt of lightning. Her gaze travelled the length of Heather's body and stopped when it met Heather's questioning blue eyes. She nodded her agreement and forced herself to look away.

Apparently, the game was over. The players had already returned to the locker room and the stadium was nearly empty. Andrea had been so affected by Heather that she hadn't noticed the game end. She glanced at the scoreboard, which read 31-7 for the visiting team.

She dared to look back over at Heather and prayed for composure. Heather had mercifully removed the jersey and sat there smiling knowingly at her.

"I guess the game is over," Andrea said dejectedly. She didn't care about the game anymore, but the fact that it was over meant that her time alone with Heather was also over. "We should probably get going."

Andrea stood, pulled Heather to her feet, and guided them very gingerly to the car. Andrea thought of excuses to prolong their time together, but she could think of nothing that wouldn't cause Rebecca to question Heather's tardiness.

She was surprised when Heather suggested they stop somewhere for a coffee.

"Won't Rebecca be waiting for you?" Andrea asked sincerely.

"Probably, but she'll get over it," Heather assured.

About a block away from the car, they stumbled upon a quaint little coffee shop and were delighted to find a quiet table near the window. Andrea struggled with the uncomfortable silence between them. She still had a lot of questions for Heather. She wanted to know about Donna. She wanted to understand Heather's relationship with Rebecca. How did Heather, who was terrified of heights, end up being a flight attendant? She wanted to know everything that made Heather who she was today.

"Your friends showed me a picture of Donna," Andrea said nonchalantly, trying to bring up the topic gently.

Heather's face flushed with shame. She knew Donna would come up eventually, but she hadn't wrapped her head around the whole Donna thing yet, and wasn't prepared to discuss her with Andie.

When Heather didn't answer, Andrea tried a more direct approach. "Where did you meet her? What was she like? Did you love her? Tell me about her, Heather."

"Look Andie, I know how it must seem. Since you saw her picture, you know she looked just like you. And yes, that was why I was originally drawn to her; in fact when I met her, on a flight from Paris, I thought she was you, until she started talking to me." Heather paused and took a sip of her coffee.

"The truth is, even though the resemblance was there, she was nothing like you. It pains me to think that maybe I used her to remember you—to fill the void you left. But I did love her. I cared about her deeply, but she wasn't you. I hated myself sometimes for wanting her to be like you," Heather said shamefully.

Andrea didn't know what to say. What could she say? Heather had to find a way to forgive herself before she would ever be able to let go of her guilt. The silence between them grew again until Heather took their conversation to a less emotional topic.

"Justine's moving out in a couple of weeks. She's moving in with her fiancé, which means, I'm going to have to start looking for another roommate," she let out a frustrated sigh.

"That's not the easiest thing to do. Besides the fact that we live so far away from civilization, there's the whole lesbian thing, which a lot of people can't accept."

"I can help with the bills, Heather," Andrea offered, though she knew Heather wouldn't accept.

"I can't let you do that, Andie. You've already paid your share of the rent and bills. I can't let you pay any more."

Andie's brain shifted into problem solving mode. Her thoughts drifted to Tammy, who had her own home, and then to Jamie, who lived in a cramped apartment, which she didn't like. "I might know someone," Andrea implied. "Give me a few days."

Out of curiosity, Andrea asked, "Why doesn't Rebecca give up her apartment?"

"That's a loaded question," Heather answered with a crooked grin. "The easiest explanation is that her apartment is much closer to her work, but the truth is …" The rest of her explanation died on her lips. What was the truth exactly?

"The truth is what?" Andrea pushed on.

"I don't know. Things between Rebecca and I are … complicated. We just sort of ended up in bed together after Donna died and things haven't really progressed beyond that."

"You aren't in love with her," Andrea said as more of a question then a statement.

Heather couldn't meet her eyes. She stared into her nearly empty coffee cup and said, "No."

"Why are you still together, then?"

After a moment of silence, Heather replied, "Convenience ... loneliness ... all the wrong reasons. Believe me ... I've been doing a lot of thinking about my relationship with Rebecca. As strange as it is, it works for us, and I don't want to end it without making sure it's the right thing to do."

Andrea understood strange relationships, and how different things worked for different people, but she couldn't help but feel hopeful that Heather might soon be single. Part of her wanted to encourage Heather to end her relationship with Rebecca, but she knew that would be wrong. This was something Heather had to do on her own terms and if that meant Andrea had to wait weeks, months, even years, she would do it. The situation she was in was her own fault, wasn't it?

Andrea looked out the window at the quickly darkening sky, drained her coffee cup, and said, "We'd better get home."

"My parent's are coming over for Thanksgiving," Heather mentioned during the drive home.

"That will be nice," Andrea said casually.

"Do you have any plans?"

"No. Why? Do you need some help?" Andrea offered.

"Well, I could use some help with dinner, since Rebecca's not much help in the kitchen, but I'd really like for you to join us ... it would be like old times."

Old times. How Andrea longed to relive some of those wonderful times. She knew she would feel like the third wheel, actually the fifth wheel, what with Rebecca still there and everything. The fact that Heather was still counting on Rebecca being around at Thanksgiving was somewhat of a blow, but if Heather wanted Andrea there, she would swallow her pride and join them for dinner.

"Would you mind if I invited Tammy?" Andrea asked. "We really are just friends, you know. And I think if you give her a chance, you might just like her."

"I don't mind at all. I owe her an apology for the way I behaved that day, anyway."

"Heather, do your parents know I live with you?" Andrea asked.

"I mentioned it casually, when I invited them."

Andrea could only imagine what Heather's parents thought of her now. At one time, they had been closer to her than her own parents had, but she had done a terrible thing to their daughter, and she wondered if they would be able to forgive her.

"Where have you guys been?" Rebecca asked when the two of them walked into the house three hours later then they should have.

"We stopped for a coffee," Heather explained defensively.

"I missed you," Rebecca said before pulling Heather into her arms and kissing her lightly on the lips.

Heather awkwardly pushed Rebecca away, almost revolted by her closeness.

Andrea watched the exchange curiously for a few moments before heading for the safety of her bedroom.

"Did you have a good time?" Rebecca asked as she pulled Heather to her again.

"I did," Heather replied and forced herself to relax into Rebecca's embrace.

Chapter 16

Heather darted across the room to answer the ringing telephone.

"Hello," she said breathlessly.

"Heather? Hi, it's Terri. I'm sorry to bother you, but I really need to get in touch with Andrea and she's not answering her cell."

"She's sleeping, Terri. Something went wrong at the plant last night and she didn't get home until a few hours ago."

"It's really important, Heather. I wouldn't have called otherwise," Terri insisted.

"I'll go wake her, but if she gets mad, I'm blaming you."

Heather anxiously walked over to Andrea's bedroom door and knocked gently before opening it.

"Andie," Heather called quietly.

The sound of Heather's voice instantly pulled Andrea out of her deep sleep. She sat up abruptly and the sheet that was covering her naked breasts fell into her lap. She struggled to cover herself as her eyes adjusted to the light.

"What's wrong," Andrea asked. It was unusual for anyone, particularly Heather, to be in her bedroom.

"Terri's on the phone," Heather replied before handing the phone over to Andrea. She made a move toward the door, but Andrea motioned for her to stay.

Whatever Terri wanted, Andrea wanted to make sure that Heather understood that nothing was going on between them. She wanted Heather to hear her end of the conversation.

"Hey, Ter, what's going on?" Andrea asked groggily.

"I'm sorry to bother you, Andrea, but there were a couple of police officers here looking for you. They wouldn't tell me what they wanted, but they left their cards and asked me to have you call them if I heard from you," Terri said.

"The police?" Andrea questioned in disbelief.

"Yes, the police. Do you want the phone number?"

"Give me five minutes to wake up and have a cup of coffee and I'll call you back, okay?"

She disconnected the call and met Heather's questioning gaze.

"The police are looking for me, and before you ask, I don't know why."

"I'll go start a pot of coffee while you get dressed," Heather offered as she left the room.

She wondered if Andrea was hungry and walked back into the room to ask without knocking. Andrea was standing beside the bed, stark naked. Andrea quickly covered what appeared to be a tattoo with the t-shirt in her hand.

Wow, Heather thought to herself. She had seen the top half a couple of months ago when Andie was sick and had been impressed by that. Seeing the entire package was almost too much. She struggled to keep herself from running into Andie's arms.

"Sorry, Andie. I just wanted to know if you were hungry," she said shyly as she averted her eyes and looked down at her feet.

"Was that a tattoo, I saw?" Heather asked. Her curiosity over the tattoo was helping to diminish her initial arousal at seeing Andie's gorgeous naked body.

"I'm hungry, but I'm too nervous to eat. I wonder what they want?" she asked calmly, not at all embarrassed by her nakedness. If it wasn't for the tattoo, she didn't want Heather to see, she would have just stayed that way. Instead, she turned away from Heather and pulled a long t-shirt over her head, which covered it.

"You should eat something. I'll make you some toast. You didn't answer my question though."

"What question was that?" Andrea asked as she brushed past Heather on the way to her dresser to find some shorts.

"Do you have a tattoo?"

"Yes."

"May I see it?"

"No."

"Why?"

"Listen Heather, can we talk about this later. It's not a good time," Andrea replied sternly.

Heather felt the tears forming in her eyes.

"I'm sorry, I won't bring it up again," Heather said as she rushed out of the bedroom.

Fuck, Andrea whispered in frustration.

"Heather, wait!"

Andrea caught up with her in the living room. She hadn't meant to make her cry, but it really wasn't the time to get into the story of how, when, and why she got her tattoo. She pulled Heather around to face her, wiped the tears from her cheeks and lifted her shirt, exposing the letter H surrounded by a heart, just above her left hipbone. Heather stepped forward and traced over the tattoo with her fingertip.

"When did you get it?" Heather asked.

"It was the first thing I did when I got off the plane in Chicago," Andrea admitted shyly.

The phone rang again, startling both women. Andrea lowered her shirt and answered the phone.

"Hello," she said almost angrily.

"Sorry, Andrea. I was trying to wait, but I'm headed into a meeting and didn't want to miss your call," Terri said apologetically.

"It's okay. Just let me grab a pen."

Andrea walked over to the sofa table and jotted down the information Terri was reading to her. Heather handed her a cup of coffee and stood silently, wondering if Andie wanted her to stay or leave. Andrea mouthed a thank-you and motioned for her to sit on the couch.

"Thanks, Ter, I'll let you know what happens."

Andrea walked over to the couch and sat down next to Heather.

"Are you in a hurry to be somewhere?" Andrea asked nervously.

"No."

"Will you sit with me while I make this call?"

"Whatever you need, Andie."

Andrea recognized Detective Donovan's name as the younger detective who responded to the call at her house the day her mother was attacked and decided to call him. She nervously dialed his number and waited.

"Donovan," he answered on the fourth ring.

"Detective Donovan, this is Andrea Reynolds. I understand you've been looking for me."

"Miss Reynolds, you're a very hard person to track down," he admitted.

"I'm not used to being looked for," she replied jokingly.

"Miss Reynolds, we've been trying to locate you to inform you that your father passed away."

"When? How?" she asked in disbelief, taking Heather's hand into hers for strength.

"Nearly two weeks ago, of a massive heart attack. Since you are listed as his next of kin, his body has been kept at the morgue waiting for instructions from you."

"What are my options?" she asked coldly. She didn't care what they did with his body.

"I apologize if this sounds insensitive, but I remember you, Miss Reynolds, and you strike me as the type of person who would just want to get this over with as quickly and painlessly as possible."

"Your assumption is correct," she replied coldly. "Just tell me what I have to do."

"If you want, you could donate his body to science. You would just have to come in and sign some paperwork."

"I'm out of state. Is there any way I could handle this from here?"

"I'm afraid not, Miss Reynolds. In light of the situation, the paperwork would have to be handled here."

She considered her options, decided she wanted to get this over with quickly, and said, "I'll be there tomorrow afternoon, if something changes, I'll call you. Thank you Detective."

Andrea disconnected from the call and stared at the phone in her hand. It just wasn't possible. Her father was supposed to suffer in prison for years for what he had done to her mother; instead, he died a quick, nearly painless death. She didn't even get a chance to tell him how she felt about him.

"Are you okay?" Heather asked after a few minutes of silence.

"I'm fine," Andrea lied. "Do you have to work tomorrow?"

"Yes, why?"

"No reason ... I have to go make some phone calls," Andrea said as she stood up and started walking toward her bedroom.

Heather sat for a few minutes trying to make sense of what was happening. Hearing only Andrea's end of the conversation wasn't much help. She knew one thing for sure.—Andie wasn't fine. She was definitely upset about something and Heather was determined to find out what it was. She called Rebecca and told her not to bother coming over later because she had plans. After a lot of grumbling, Rebecca agreed to stay home.

Andrea called the airline to book a flight to Cincinnati, she called Terri and asked her if she could pick her up at the airport around eleven, then called Carlos to tell him she wouldn't be in for a couple of days. Now that all the details had been handled, her brain was able to register the reality of the situation. She was sitting on her bed sobbing when Heather walked in.

"Oh, Andie, come here," Heather said as she sat on the bed, leaned against the pillows, and held her arms open in invitation. After a few minutes, Andrea's tears subsided and she relaxed into Heather's arms.

"My dad died, and I didn't get a chance to tell him how much I hated him."

"I'm sure he knew, Andie." She caressed Andrea's face and wiped away the tears.

"I thought you'd be happy he was dead," Heather said sympathetically.

"He didn't suffer enough. He should have suffered the way my mom did. It's not fair. He was dead before he even knew what hit him."

"I'm sorry, Andie. I feel so bad for you. Is there anything I can do?"

"Can you sit with me for a while? I'm so tired, but I'm afraid to fall asleep."

"I'll be right here," Heather assured.

Heather kissed her softly on the forehead. She remembered the terrible nightmares Andrea used to have. It was so painful to watch her relive that day. She wished she could somehow erase it from her mind forever.

Andrea fell asleep after only a few minutes. She was exhausted, mentally and physically. Heather's warm embrace made her feel safe and comfortable like it always had. After eight years, she was finally home again. Heather's arms were her home, her safe place. No one could hurt her there.

Heather watched Andrea sleep peacefully for nearly an hour before she saw the signs of the nightmare coming on. She remembered the signs. The breathing changes. The slight facial expression alterations. The minute movements and twitches of her extremities. She knew what would come next, and it pained her to watch Andrea's peaceful sleep be transformed into a violent memory of terror.

Heather pulled her arms tightly around Andrea, knowing it was pointless to wake her until the nightmare was over. She sobbed when Andrea cried out and struggled in her arms. The sweat, the tears, the cries for help. It was overwhelming. Heather willed the nightmare to pass quickly. She wished that she could take away Andie's pain. Heather felt helpless, useless. There was nothing more she could do but hold her and pray for it to be over quickly.

"No!" Andrea shouted. Her eyes were open and wild with anger.

"Andie! Wake up! It's me," Heather tried to reason with her and bring her out of the nightmare.

"Andie!" she shouted again when Andrea freed herself and raised her arm to strike her.

"Andie, it's me, Heather," she said desperately as she steeled herself for the blow.

Heather's name brought Andrea to a state of full consciousness.

"Heather," Andrea said in astonishment. She looked at her raised fist, then back at Heather and cried, "I'm so sorry. You're crying. Oh my God! Did I hurt you?" She frantically examined Heather's beautiful face for any signs of injury.

"You didn't, Andie. It's okay," Heather said and pulled her close. She caressed her face and held her while she cried.

"Thank you," Andrea whispered, her head resting softly in Heather's lap.

She felt like a child. Weak and helpless. She was ashamed and scared. Heather would never want her like this. She had witnessed the fear in Heather's eyes. Would she really have struck her? She didn't trust herself. She let Heather go and stood up abruptly.

"I'm going to take a shower," she said assertively.

"Andie, it's okay. I don't think you'd ever hurt me."

"I can't take that chance, Heather."

"I can. Go take a shower and I'll make you something to eat."

Andrea knew by the tone in Heather's voice that there was no point trying to argue with her. She would try to reason with her later. In her heart, she knew that if she ever did anything to hurt Heather, she would never get over it. It was too risky right now. Maybe in a few weeks, after some sessions with Dr. Cochran, she'd be able to regain some control over her nightmares again. For now though, it was too dangerous for Heather.

Andrea picked at her food and pushed it around her plate with her fork. She had no appetite, but Heather insisted she eat something. She managed to choke down a few bites under Heather's watchful eye, and then pushed the plate away.

"Heather, I ..."

"No, Andie. Listen to me. I'm not going to let you push me away. Whether you want to admit it or not, you need me. Even if you had hit me, I'd still be sitting here because I'd know it wasn't me you were hitting. I hate what you're going through. It hurts me to see you like that. I feel so helpless. Let me do what little I can to help you," Heather pleaded.

"You can't be with me all the time, Heather. You have Rebecca. I have to get through this on my own," Andrea insisted.

"Rebecca's not coming over tonight so you're stuck with me. If you're that worried about it, I'll sleep in the chair," she offered.

"I can't ask you to do that, you have to work tomorrow. You need your rest."

"You didn't ask me. I offered, and I'm tired of this conversation. There's nothing you can do or say to change my mind, so let it go."

Andrea glared at her in defeat, unable to find a sound argument to justify her concerns. Heather always did win when they argued; she should have remembered that and saved her breath.

"I don't think you should go to Cincinnati by yourself," Heather added.

"Terri's picking me up at the airport."

"Good," Heather managed. She wished she had the day off so that she would know Andie was okay, but she also knew that Terri was more than capable of giving Andie what she needed.

Later that night, after Andie fell asleep, Heather quietly slipped into bed beside her. She watched her sleep for hours, wondering if Andie would ever be able to share the pain she felt. Andrea surprisingly slept through the night. Each time Andrea rustled in her sleep, Heather would wake up and watch over her. Thankfully, none of the nightmares seemed as violent as the one she had that afternoon.

When the alarm clock sounded just after six in the morning, Andrea hit the snooze button, stretched, and rolled over right into Heather's waiting arms.

"What do you think you're doing?" she asked angrily.

"I was cold," Heather said lamely, trying to find a reasonable excuse for having broken her promise to sleep in the chair.

"We had an agreement," Andrea argued.

"Andie, what's the big deal? Nothing happened."

"But what if it had?"

"It didn't!" Heather insisted angrily. She didn't care about what ifs and could haves. She did what she thought was right and there was nothing Andie could say to change the way she felt.

Andrea let out a frustrated breath, got out of bed, walked into the bathroom, and slammed the door shut behind her.

Heather chuckled even though there was nothing funny about the situation. She knew Andie had given up and that she had won the argument. She spent a few minutes cuddling Andie's still-warm pillow and allowing her senses to be filled with Andie's lingering scent. As soon as she heard the water shut off, she scampered out of the room and into her own.

When she emerged from her room an hour later, dressed for work, Andie was already gone. She said a silent prayer asking God to give Andie the strength to make it through this day and to find some closure and peace within herself before she returned.

Chapter 17

Terri looked at Andrea curiously, as she approached the car. She had never seen her look so defeated, so hollow, and so scared. It pained her to see Andrea like that. She didn't know all of the details, but Andrea had filled her in on some of it when she called. She couldn't begin to comprehend what Andrea was feeling, but she wanted to. Terri knew in her heart that Heather was the only person Andrea would confide in, but Heather wasn't there, so she'd have to try. She wanted to try.

The plan was for Andrea to drop her back off at work before heading to the police station, but after seeing her in person, Terri immediately called the office and told them she wouldn't be returning today. She had to be there for her when she was ready to talk about it. She hoped Andrea would let her in.

"This isn't the way to the office," Andrea said as they drove down the interstate.

"I'm going with you, Reynolds. You shouldn't be alone."

"I'm fine. I don't need a babysitter. I just need a car."

"I'm going. I won't change my mind, so don't even try," Terri insisted.

Andrea suddenly realized that it was just as pointless to try to argue with Terri, as it was to try to argue with Heather. She thought back to some of the other women she dated and tried to remember if they were just as strong-willed. She couldn't remember any that were. Maybe that's why she and Terri got along so well. In that way, Terri reminded her of Heather. It was a strange and unexpected realization.

She took a deep breath when they arrived at the police station. Terri pulled her into an embrace and held her for several minutes before saying, "Let's get this over with."

Andrea put on what she thought was a brave face as they entered the ominous looking building. She felt anything but brave. She was terrified, and having to walk into a police station, even when you weren't in trouble was a little bit disconcerting. Subconsciously, there was always that fear that you had done something wrong that you couldn't remember, or that you'd be mistaken for a criminal and be arrested on the spot. She was happy Terri decided to go with her; she wasn't sure she'd have been able to do this alone.

On the drive over, Andrea had explained in greater detail, the reason for this trip. Prior to that, the only thing Terri knew was that Andrea's father had killed her mother and that he had died in prison. She had never asked for more details because she could tell how much it hurt Andrea to talk about it.

Rather than wait for the dangerous looking elevator, they climbed the three flights of stairs, which brought them to the fourth floor, where Detective Donovan's cubicle could be found. The air was thick and musty smelling. The stale stench of cigarette smoke was still prominent after years of being a smoke-free building.

Andrea easily recognized Detective Donovan, who sat at his desk with a telephone pressed to his ear. He had lost a little hair and gained a few pounds, but his blue eyes were still as compassionate and understanding as they had been that terrible day.

When he stood to greet her, rather than offer his hand, he pulled her into a comforting hug. Terri sat quietly as Andrea and the Detective took care of the paperwork. He handed Andrea an envelope, which contained her father's personal possessions, looked at her with a great deal of compassion, and said, "You have to find a way to forgive him."

Andrea must have looked at him strangely because he continued.

"Miss Reynolds, you must think I've lost my mind, but I assure you, my situation was not so very different from your own. The difference for me was that my father killed my baby sister. He was drunk and she wouldn't stop crying, so he threw her across the room. She was only eight months old." As he spoke, his eyes remained fixed on the wall behind them. It was as if he was recalling a case he had worked on as opposed to his own memories. Maybe that detachment was what got him through the day. His eyes met Andrea's.

"Trust me, Miss Reynolds. Your father was sick. He didn't do it intentionally. You can always hate him, but you have to forgive him or you will never get on with your life."

They sat in the car in complete silence in the police station parking lot. Terri tried to come up with something to say to console Andrea, but there was nothing she could say. It wasn't something she could understand. She could not offer advice. All she could do was listen, if and when, Andrea started to speak. She had tried not to look shocked when Andrea told her about her childhood, but she knew she had failed miserably. She was seeing Andrea in a completely new light now. It was as if she was meeting her for the first time.

"Would you mind driving me out to the cemetery?" Andrea asked solemnly. She wanted to visit her mother's grave. She needed her mother. Maybe if she went to her gravesite, the answers she sought would come to her.

"I'll take you wherever you need to go," Terri replied. She would do anything for Andrea right now. Whatever she needed. Over the years she had grown to love Andrea, but not in a romantic way. It was something even deeper than that.

Terri stayed in the car so Andrea could visit her mother's grave alone. She parked close enough to keep an eye on her, but far enough away so as not to infringe on her privacy. She couldn't imagine what it was like for Andrea growing up, since her own parents had been very loving and understanding. When Terri looked back on her childhood, it was with great fondness. She couldn't remember a time where she had been anything but happy. It was something she'd taken for granted, until today. She picked up the phone and called her mother just to thank her for giving her a happy, loving home to grow up in.

It was as if Mother Nature knew this day was coming and had scripted the perfect weather conditions to enhance Andrea's dark and sullen mood. The air was a crisp thirty-eight degrees and the heavy grey clouds loomed very low to the ground. The only sound in the deserted cemetery was the occasional rustling of dry leaves as they were swept along the ground by the wind.

Andrea crouched down and busied herself with pulling the weeds that had grown around her mother's grave. The weeds only served to remind her of the guilt she felt for not visiting more often. She honestly just didn't see the point in visiting. She felt that her mother would hear her no matter where she was, but she had bought the headstone in her mother's memory and talking to it somehow made it more real.

The stone she selected was made of beautiful black granite. On it was etched a stunning photo of her mother when she was younger and full of life. The inscription simply read, "Mother."

"Hi, Mom. Sorry I haven't been here in a while," Andrea said softly.

"I guess you know why I'm here … it just doesn't seem fair." Andrea sat on the damp ground, wrapped her arms around her knees, and stared at her mother's picture.

"I live with Heather now, but I guess you know that too." She was making small talk with a tombstone. It felt strange, but she just couldn't bring herself to ask the questions she needed answers to.

"Mom, did you forgive him? I know I have to, but how? I need your help." She sat there for close to an hour, staring, praying, and waiting for answers as the snow flurries began to fall. It was one of those bizarre snow showers, where the flurries danced around crazily and never really reached the ground. Sometimes she felt like those snowflakes—caught in a whirlwind of uncertainty, floating around aimlessly, never knowing where she'd land.

Andrea didn't hear Terri approach and drape a warm jacket around her shoulders. When she turned to thank her, she had already gone back to the car. She sat for what she thought was a few minutes more as a wonderfully peaceful feeling washed over her. She glanced at her watch and realized that she wasn't going to make her return flight. She hadn't planned on being out there so long. Suddenly, she was shivering from the cold. It was almost as if she had just woke up from a dream and hadn't been able to feel anything before that moment.

She stood, looked down at her mother's beautiful face, and said, "Thanks, Mom. I miss you."

Terri had the heat cranked full blast in the car as they left the cemetery.

"Why don't you just spend the night and go home tomorrow, instead of trying to rebook your flight tonight," Terri suggested.

Andrea felt overwhelmed. She felt strangely at peace, yet unbelievable lost. She wanted to be with Heather; she needed Heather, but Terri was right—she would have a difficult, if not impossible time, trying to rebook her flight unless she booked it for tomorrow.

"Are you sure you don't mind?" Andrea asked.

"Not at all. I even have some leftover chili for dinner. Or we can go out if you want."

"I just want to go home. I'm so cold. Why did you let me stay out there so long?" Andrea asked.

"I knew you were doing what you had to do. I didn't want to rush you."

"Thanks."

Andrea was glad to have Terri in her life, even if it was just as a friend now.

"You should call Heather, so she doesn't worry about you," Terri suggested as she pulled into her driveway.

After a long moment of silence, Andrea broke down and sobbed, "I almost hit her yesterday ... I didn't mean to. I was having a nightmare ..."

Terri didn't know what was upsetting Andrea more, her father's death, or the incident with Heather. She was not equipped to deal with her in this condition.

"Do you have a therapist here in town?" Terri asked, not knowing what else to do for her. Her heart was breaking for this woman.

Andrea nodded yes.

"Why don't you call and find out if she will see you tonight or tomorrow morning," Terri suggested.

Andrea was too distraught to speak, so she found Dr. Cochran's number in her cell phone and handed it to Terri.

Upon Terri's insistence that Andrea's situation was urgent, Dr. Cochran's assistant managed to fit her in later that evening. Temporarily relieved, she led Andrea into the house and prepared a nice hot bubble bath for her before getting started on dinner.

They ate in uncomfortable silence; Terri unable to find the right words to say. She watched with great concern as Andrea moved the food around on her plate, not really eating any of it. The hour and a half until Andrea's appointment couldn't pass quickly enough.

"Do you mind if I go lie down for a little while?" Andrea asked.

"Not at all. Do you want some company?"

"Not really," Andrea replied truthfully.

Terri watched Andrea walk to the bedroom and was both relieved and saddened. She was happy to not have the pressure of trying to console her for a few minutes, but she also felt bad that it seemed even Andrea knew that she couldn't help her.

Andrea sat on the bed, not the least bit tired. She just couldn't stand to see Terri looking so helpless. Andrea knew it wasn't Terri's fault. Very few people would know how to react in a situation like this.

For the first time, Andrea found the courage to open the envelope that contained her father's possessions. She dumped the contents on the bed and sorted through them. She immediately recognized his watch and wedding band. The only other items in the envelope were a comb and a letter addressed to her. It looked several years old. Maybe he didn't know where to send it since she had no fixed address. Part of her wanted to throw it away. Another part of her longed to know what he had to say.

She stared at the envelope for several minutes debating the pros and cons of opening it. On one hand, it might help her understand how he could have committed such a horrific act; on the other hand, it could contain a declaration of love and a plea for sympathy. Andrea didn't love him, nor did she want his love and sympathy was something he didn't deserve.

Two of the biggest hurdles she hadn't been able to get over were the how and why of her father's actions. How could a man, who claimed to love his wife so desperately, kill her, and why had he done it—what had she done to provoke him that day?

Shakily, she opened the envelope and began to read his words.

My dearest Andrea,
I know you will never understand what I did. I, myself, can't even begin to understand it. I was sick. I don't even remember it. I remember sitting on the back porch, not knowing how I got there—it was as if I had just woken up. I remember hearing sirens then looking down at my hands. I knew I had done something, but I didn't know what. I had a terrible feeling that whatever it was, was very bad. I peeked through the window and saw you there with the paramedics and I got scared and ran.
A few hours later, I went back to the house—I wanted to know what happened. When I saw the crime scene tape and all the blood on the floor, I knew it was bad. I didn't remember doing anything, but for some reason, I knew it was me. To this day, I still don't remember it. I turned myself in that night, for a crime I didn't remember committing. When they told me what I had done, I couldn't believe it. I loved your mother. She was the most amazing woman in the world.
I know you don't believe I loved her, but I did …

He went on to profess his love for his wife and to ask for forgiveness and understanding. Most of this Andrea ignored. She was mystified by the beginning of his letter. How could he not remember? Maybe he just didn't want to remember. She read it repeatedly and began comparing what he did to what she almost did to Heather. Was it really that different? If he didn't mean to hurt her mother and doesn't remember it, wasn't that almost the same as if she had actually hit Heather? Although the cause was different, the actions would have been the same.

Andrea was surprised to find that Dr. Cochran's home office was an exact duplicate of her downtown office. Everything, right down to the pen she was writing with, was the same. She told Andrea that it was easier for her patients to discuss their feelings if they felt comfortable and weren't focussing on the room they were in. Once inside, there was no reason to feel like you were anywhere but at her downtown office.

Andrea was surprised, that after nearly two hours of talking, Dr. Cochran hadn't asked her to leave. She never let her appointments run longer than an hour. When she was finally finished, Dr. Cochran told her she had to find a way to forgive her father. The same thing Detective Donovan had said.

"Andrea, he's gone. There's nothing you can do to hurt him now. The only one suffering here is you," Dr. Cochran said cautiously.

"When you leave here, I want you to write him a letter. Start by writing down exactly how you feel, or felt, and when you get to the end—forgive him. Keep that letter with you until you're ready to let it go. When it's time, do with it as you please; burn it, put it in a bottle and throw it in the ocean. It doesn't matter how—just release it. You'll feel better. I promise."

Andrea thought it sounded like a load of crap. How can a simple piece of paper make you feel better? She was reluctant at first, thinking it was ridiculous, but when she got back to Terri's, she stayed up most of the night and wrote her father a five-page letter. It was surprisingly easy to put her feelings down on paper. She wished she had found the courage to see him face to face before he died, so that she could have told him how she felt.

Chapter 18

Almost two weeks had passed since Andrea's trip to Cincinnati. She was feeling a lot better. Two days ago, she had burned the letter that she had written to her father just as Dr. Cochran had suggested. It was wonderfully liberating to let go of all those emotions.

She was looking forward to spending the weekend with Heather's family—as long as they had forgiven her. Holidays with Heather's family had always been the happiest times of her life. If they were still angry with her, it would be very uncomfortable. Heather was always very open and honest with her parents, so there was a good possibility that they knew exactly what she had done.

Andrea was happy to be busy in the kitchen preparing Thanksgiving dinner so she didn't have the time to worry about what Heather's parents would say to her. Thank God, she didn't have to be alone with them.

She pulled the pecan pie from the oven and glanced at the clock. Heather would be home any minute to spend a couple of hours helping her in the kitchen before heading back to the airport to pick up her parents.

"Hey, Rebecca, where's Andie?" Heather asked when Rebecca answered the phone.

"Last time I saw her, she was arguing with the turkey. Where are you?"

Heather laughed. "Who was winning, Andie or the turkey?"

"Definitely the turkey. Shouldn't you be home by now?" Rebecca questioned.

"I'm stuck in Denver. There was a big snowstorm and everything is backed up. I'm going to be a few hours late," Heather said.

"That sucks. Do you need me to do something?"

"Could you bring the phone to Andie? I really need to talk to her."

"I miss you," Rebecca said.

Heather pretended not to hear her. She didn't miss Rebecca at all. Being away from her for the last two days was the only thing that made working the holiday bearable. She waited quietly until she heard Andrea's familiar voice.

"Hello," Andrea said after Rebecca handed her the phone and left the room.

"Hey, Andie! I hear the turkey is giving you grief." Heather chuckled.

"We're okay now. We've come to an understanding," she said as she glared over at the turkey, which she had finally managed to stuff and fit into the less than adequate roasting pan.

"That's good because I need you to do me a huge favour."

Andrea could almost see Heather's innocent looking face. Her head would be tilted slightly to the right and she'd be batting her eyelashes playfully the way she always did when she wanted something. It was a look that Andrea could never deny.

"Name it!" Andrea said.

"Will you go pick my parents up at the airport? I'm going to be a couple hours late."

Andrea would gladly do anything for Heather, but the thought of seeing her parents after all this time, without Heather there to defend her, was almost frightening. What would they say to her? What would she say to them? How could she explain?

"What about Rebecca?" Andrea suggested.

"Yeah! Um ... they don't really like Rebecca," Heather said honestly.

"Do they like me right now?"

"They loved you Andie. Like one of their own. I'm sure they're over it by now. You'll be fine," Heather assured.

"I'm scared," Andrea said only half-teasing.

"Be brave, Andie! They land at one o'clock." She hung up and didn't give Andrea a chance to back out.

The airport was packed with travellers coming and going. Families were greeting each other with warm embraces and loving kisses. Andrea prayed for their flight to be delayed as she circled the parking lot, time after time, looking for a spot.

Even though she jogged to the terminal, when she reached it, almost forty-five minutes after their flight was scheduled to land, Mr. and Mrs. Johnson were standing at the curb next to four large suitcases.

How long are they staying, she wondered for a moment, and then realized that at least two of those suitcases were probably full of new clothes and other gifts for their one and only precious daughter. A daughter to whom she had done the inexcusable. The knot in her stomach tightened as she approached them.

By the look of shock on their faces, Heather had not been able to reach them to tell them that she would be picking them up.

"Andrea?" Mrs. Johnson said. "Why, you haven't changed a bit," she exclaimed.

Andrea stood there awkwardly for a few moments until Mrs. Johnson wrapped her ever-loving arms around her and pulled her close. Although she couldn't see her face, she could feel Mrs. Johnson crying in her arms.

"Oh! Dear! Look at me, I'm a mess," Mrs. Johnson said, trying not to show her embarrassment. "It must be the holidays. I always get emotional around the holidays." She dabbed her eyes with a tissue.

"You guys look terrific," Andrea said sincerely. Florida suited these people well. Their bronzed skin glowed with a healthy sheen. They looked better than they had eight years ago.

"It's good to see you, Mr. Johnson," Andrea said as he shook her offered hand graciously. "Heather's flight got delayed by a couple of hours, so she asked me to pick you up. I hope you don't mind."

"There's nobody else we'd rather have picked us up, Andrea," Mrs. Johnson said convincingly.

"Especially not that good for nothing sponge our daughter's been dating," Mr. Johnson mumbled under his breath, earning him a sharp elbow to the ribs from his wife.

When Heather walked into the house several hours later, she found Rebecca sitting silently beside her father watching football and her mother in the kitchen, working on dinner with Andie. It felt both awkward and familiar. Andie should be sitting out here with her father, and she should be in the kitchen helping her mother. That's the way it used to be. But things were different now, weren't they?

"Hi, Daddy!" Heather said innocently. She wrapped her arms around his neck the way she always had, and filled his face with kisses.

"How's my baby girl?" he asked. No matter how old Heather was, she'd always be his baby girl.

"Tired. I hate working the holidays. Was Andie late picking you up?"

"No. She was right on time," he lied. No matter what Andrea did, she'd always be the only one good enough for his daughter. "She's in the kitchen helping your mother with dinner," he said, wanting her in the kitchen with Andrea, and away from this Rebecca creature, as soon as possible.

Heather stood, but before she could escape to the kitchen, Rebecca stood as well, and planted a kiss on her lips. "I missed you," Rebecca said seductively.

Heather gave her a stern look, telling her to behave in front of her parents. She considered, for an instant on the way to the kitchen, that she probably wouldn't mind if Andie kissed her in front of her parents.

Heather stopped in the doorway and watched in awe as her mother and Andie stood side by side working away diligently on peeling potatoes. The sight brought tears to her eyes. This house finally felt like home.

"Hi, Mom!" She greeted her mother with a warm hug.

"Thanks for picking them up, Andie."

"No problem. Did your dad tell you how late I was?" Andrea figured Mr. Johnson would probably be grumbling a little bit about her being so late.

"How late were you? He said you were right on time," Heather accused.

"Our flight must have been late," Mrs. Johnson interrupted, knowing how much her husband adored Andrea.

"We really didn't wait long at all," she added despite the fact that their flight had actually been early and they waited over an hour.

Andrea gave her a puzzled look, but went right on peeling potatoes as the other two women talked.

A few minutes later, Andrea glanced at the clock and said, "Tammy's going to be here soon. Do you mind if I leave the two of you to this and go get ready?"

Mrs. Johnson looked at her disapprovingly while Heather said, "Go on, Andie, we've got this."

Once Andrea had left the kitchen, Heather's mother immediately began with the questions.

"Who's Tammy?" she asked critically.

"Just a friend of Andie's," Heather replied casually.

"Are you sure she's just a friend?"

"I'm positive, Mom. What does it matter anyway?"

"I thought you and Andrea had patched up your differences?"

"We did. Does that mean she's not allowed to have other friends?"

"I don't know, Heather. Listen to me going on and on about Andrea. How are you? You must be exhausted."

Andrea greeted Tammy at the door with a friendly hug.

"Here," Tammy said as she held out two bottles. "A bottle of wine for them, and a bottle of sparkling grape juice for us."

"Thanks, Tammy, you didn't have to bring anything though." She looked at Tammy thoughtfully.

"You look … different?"

"Do I?" Tammy teased.

"It's not your hair, or your clothes. Why do you look so different?"

"I'll tell you later. Are you going to let me in?"

"Sorry. Come on in, I'll introduce you."

She walked with Tammy over to the couch and began the introductions.

"Sir, this is my friend, Tammy. Tammy, I'd like you to meet Heather's father, Mr. Johnson."

"It's a pleasure to meet you, sir. I don't know your daughter very well, but I can see where she gets those amazing blue eyes."

"Ah! Flattery will get you everywhere, but you haven't met her mother yet. Heather is the spitting image of her mother at that age."

They turned their attention to Rebecca.

"Tammy, this is Rebecca, Heather's … girlfriend," she managed to say through gritted teeth. "Rebecca, this is my friend Tammy."

"Hey," Rebecca said casually and turned her attention back to the television set.

Andrea ushered Tammy into the kitchen and made introductions there as well. A short while later, the six of them gathered around the table while Mr. Johnson said grace. It was the conclusion that caught Andrea off guard.

"And Lord, more than anything, thank you for bringing all of my girls together again. Amen."

"This turkey is wonderful, Andrea. And you'll just have to give me the recipe for this dressing. It's fantastic," Mrs. Johnson cooed, causing Rebecca to roll her eyes in disgust.

Rebecca couldn't understand why Heather's parents kept fawning over Andrea while they continued to treat her so poorly. She had always assumed that they just couldn't accept the fact that their daughter was a lesbian—apparently, it was her they didn't like. She'd have to do something to win them over.

"Actually, Mrs. Johnson, it's your recipe. I just added a secret ingredient," Andrea said truthfully. She watched as Heather's mother savoured the flavour trying to identify what the secret ingredient was.

"Tammy, has Jamie mentioned anything to you about taking the room here now that Justine's moved out?" Andrea asked.

"Actually, as it turns out, Jamie's going to be moving in with me," she said shyly as a blush crept across her face.

Andrea suddenly realized why Tammy looked different. She was absolutely glowing. They had talked about her feelings for Jamie and Andrea had encouraged Tammy to tell Jamie before it was too late. She must have followed Andrea's advice. She lifted her glass to Tammy and said, "Congratulations!" No one else even seemed to be paying attention to their conversation except for Rebecca, who had the oddest expression on her face.

"Heather," Rebecca said, "I've been thinking. Since Justine is gone, maybe it's time I give up my apartment and move in here permanently."

Mrs. Johnson coughed loudly as she choked on the bite of food that refused to be swallowed, after hearing Rebecca's announcement. Heather looked at Andrea in a desperate plea before downing the contents of her wine glass in one gulp. Mr. Johnson chuckled to himself, finding the whole situation quite entertaining. Tammy sat there as all the pieces to the Andrea puzzle started falling into place.

"Does anyone want coffee?" Heather asked as she stood from the table, looking for any excuse to get away.

"Yes, dear, coffee would be lovely," Mrs. Johnson replied, as did Mr. Johnson and Tammy.

After a few minutes, Tammy nudged Andrea's knee and motioned for her to go help Heather in the kitchen.

"Excuse me," Andrea said as she stood. "I'll go help Heather with the coffee."

Heather was starting at the empty coffee pot when Andrea walked in.

"Hey, that came out of nowhere," Andrea said.

"What is she thinking? Can't she tell I've been pushing her away lately? What am I going to do?" Heather cried.

Andrea pulled her into her arms and held her.

"It's going to be okay. Just get through this weekend and then sit her down and tell her the truth. I promise, it will be okay," Andrea assured her as she stroked her long blond hair.

Mrs. Johnson stepped into the kitchen and cleared her throat loudly to announce herself.

"How's the coffee coming along, girls?"

Heather stepped out of Andrea's comforting embrace, looked at her mother and defensively said, "She's just helping me make the coffee."

"I see that," her mother replied. "But you might actually want to put some water in that pot unless you're expecting it to magically appear."

"I'll go start clearing the table," Andrea offered and disappeared from the kitchen in a flash.

"Heather, forgive me for asking you this, but why is Rebecca even here?" her mother asked.

"She's my girlfriend, why wouldn't she be here?"

"I mean, why is she still your girlfriend? The two of you don't belong together."

"I know. It just never seems to be the right time. I promise, after this weekend I'm going to end things with her."

"Good," her mother replied just as Andrea came back into the kitchen, arms full of plates, with Tammy in tow.

"Everything okay in here?" Andrea asked cautiously.

"Just peachy," Heather replied sarcastically.

Chapter 19

A few hours later, after Tammy had gone home, Andrea was helping Mrs. Johnson with the final clean up of the kitchen. Things were going well and Andrea had let go of the notion that Heather's parents might confront her about what she had done to their daughter.

"Andrea, you know what you did to my daughter was despicable," Mrs. Johnson started to say.

Here we go, Andrea thought. She shouldn't have allowed herself to relax. Just when she thought it was safe to be alone with them, Mrs. Johnson wielded her sword.

"Do you know how many times I had to sit on the phone, hundreds of miles away, and listen to her cry? I felt useless. I couldn't take my daughter's pain away."

Andrea stood silently. It was clear Mrs. Johnson wanted to finish what she had to say before allowing Andrea to defend herself.

"It's going to take a lot of happiness to make up for all of that pain," she said and finally allowed Andrea to respond.

"Yes, ma'am, I know." It was the only acceptable response. She hadn't been given the opening she needed to defend herself.

"If my daughter does as she has promised, and asks Rebecca to leave, are you going to step up and take control of this relationship? It's clear to me that the two of you still love each other a great deal. One of you has to move things along and I don't think Heather is strong enough to do it. She's terrified of being rejected by you," Mrs. Johnson said almost angrily.

Andrea took a deep breath and considered her response for several moments before answering. She felt like she was being scolded by one of her own parents. Her relationship with Heather's parents created a strange dynamic—if she and Heather were a couple, they would be both her parents and her in-laws. It would require a difficult balancing act to continue.

"If Heather ends her relationship with Rebecca, I promise I will do what I can to win back her trust and her love," Andrea assured.

"I expect that the only tears my daughter sheds for you, from this point on, will be tears of joy," Mrs. Johnson said with authority.

"I understand," Andrea replied nervously.

"Good. Now, what was that secret ingredient in the dressing?" Mrs. Johnson asked, decidedly ending the discussion.

Andrea let out a sigh of relief and said, "Love."

That wasn't so bad, she thought to herself on her way out of the kitchen with a beer for Mr. Johnson.

"Andrea, come sit with me for a few minutes. I'd like to talk to you about something," Mr. Johnson said.

Andrea swallowed nervously. She had just gone through this with Heather's mother; now, she was going to go through it again with her father. Where the hell were Heather and Rebecca anyhow? Heather wasn't supposed to leave her alone with her parents.

"Sir," she started nervously. "Your wife just gave me a stern talking to."

"Yeah, yeah!" he replied. "Hurt feelings, broken hearts, blah, blah, blah. Do you know what went though my mind when I realized that my daughter was a lesbian?"

Andrea gave him a puzzled look.

"What about my grandchildren? That's all I could think about. I don't care who my daughter sleeps with as long as she's happy, but I want grandchildren. I felt cheated somehow. What fun is it to grow old if you don't have grandchildren to spoil?"

Andrea began to sweat. She thought she had prepared herself for anything Heather's parents could throw her way, but this was something totally unexpected.

"Grandchildren, sir?"

"Yes, Andrea. Are you prepared to help my daughter raise my grandchildren?" He had the most serious look on his face and Andrea realized that he wasn't joking. She hadn't thought about having children one way or another. She honestly hadn't thought past the hug they shared in the kitchen during dinner. Children just seemed like such a stretch from where her relationship with Heather was right now. How could she even begin to think about having children with a woman she wasn't even dating?

"Sir, you do realize that your daughter is still dating Rebecca, right?"

"Minor technicality." He waved his hand in the air dismissively. "It's you she loves. It's just a matter of time."

Andrea shook her head in disbelief. Mr. Johnson never failed to speak his mind. He'd say it as he saw it and didn't care one bit what other people thought.

"*If* things work out between Heather and me, and *if* she wants children," she added cautiously, "I will do whatever it takes to make that happen."

"Good. How 'bout those Patriots this year?" he said, indicating that the conversation was over.

Rebecca and Heather sat in the glider outside on the porch. Millions of stars were twinkling in the dark night sky. Heather couldn't wait until next week; she couldn't wait another hour. She had to end her relationship with Rebecca now. Although she didn't want to cause a scene and disrupt Thanksgiving for her family, she thought that at least they'd be around to offer her support if things didn't end well.

"Listen, Rebecca, I appreciate your offer to move in here and everything, but I think it's time we move on. You deserve to be happy and I can't make you happy anymore. I value our friendship, but I just can't keep doing this," Heather said as gently as possible.

"Are you sure this is what you want?" Rebecca asked.

"Yes, I'm sure."

"Okay. If that's what you want ... I'll miss you though," Rebecca said sincerely as she stood.

"You don't have to leave right this minute," Heather said, even though she wanted nothing more than for Rebecca to leave.

"Yes I do. I think I'll drive out and spend the rest of the weekend with my folks. I'll stop by next week to pick up my things," Rebecca replied sadly. She hugged Heather and walked away.

That was too easy, Heather thought, but shrugged it off and went back into the house to tell her family the good news.

This isn't over, Rebecca said to herself as she got in her car. This had something to do with Andrea and she'd be damned if she was going to let Andrea steal her girl. She would win Heather back, or at the very least, make sure she didn't end up with Andrea.

Andrea watched with a glimmer of hope, as Rebecca's car sped out of the driveway. Heather was supposed to wait until after the holiday to end their relationship. Something must have happened to cause her to change her mind. Rebecca clearly didn't look happy when she left. When Heather reappeared a few minutes later, she looked relieved.

"She's gone," she said almost happily, as if a great weight had been lifted from her shoulders.

Andrea thought she saw a hint of concern on Heather's face as she told her parents the good news.

"I'm so proud of you, dear," Mrs. Johnson said.

"It's about damn time," mumbled Mr. Johnson.

"Daddy!" Heather exclaimed in disbelief. She knew her parents never cared for Rebecca, but she didn't realize how strongly they felt about her.

"Rebecca was good for me. She helped me a lot after Donna died."

"She helped you spend your money," he shot back.

"Come on, honey. It's late. Let's get to bed and leave these two alone to talk," suggested Mrs. Johnson.

Andrea fought the urge to drag Heather to her room to show her exactly how she felt about her. Despite the fact that Heather seemed happy to be rid of Rebecca, it would be very gauche to jump right in as if Rebecca hadn't still been Heather's girlfriend only a couple of hours ago. Heather could have been putting on a brave face in front of her parents so they didn't worry. She might truly be upset.

"How are you holding up?" Andrea asked as she and Heather sat on the couch.

"I'm okay. I'm glad she's gone. I've just got this feeling that …" The rest of her thought died on her lips. She didn't want Andrea to be concerned about something that was little more than a gut feeling. It wasn't as if Rebecca had said anything to suggest she might cause a problem. It was what she didn't say that concerned her.

"You have a feeling that what?" Andrea questioned.

"It's nothing really. So tell me, did my parents give you the third degree? I was worried about leaving you alone with them for so long," Heather said, decidedly changing the subject.

"We had a little chat. It wasn't nearly as bad as I expected."

"Well that's good. I told you they loved you. I knew they couldn't stay angry with you," Heather said.

"What about you, Heather? Are you still angry with me?"

"No, Andie. I forgave you a long time ago," Heather replied as she walked toward her bedroom. "I'm going to bed. It's been a long day."

"Goodnight, Heather."

Heather paused in front of her bedroom door before going in.

"Andie, in case you're wondering, it's not just my parents who love you," she admitted before rushing into her room and closing the door behind her.

Andrea stared at Heather's closed bedroom door in disbelief. "I love you too, Heather," she said softly.

Even though she knew Heather didn't hear her, it felt good just to say the words. Despite the fact that she was looking forward to spending the rest of the weekend with Heather and her parents, she couldn't wait until they were gone so they'd get a chance to be alone and talk.

Tomorrow, the four of them would spend the day in the kitchen baking cookies. The next day, Heather would go shopping with her mother and leave Andrea home to watch football with her father. That was something she was looking forward to. The two of them used to be very close. Watching football with him was a Thanksgiving tradition. She'd never let them know how much it had bothered her to see Rebecca sitting with him earlier.

Their return flight to Florida coincided with Heather's work schedule so they would be leaving with her when she went to work on Sunday. Since Justine moved out, Heather was working more hours, so there was no telling when they'd get a chance to be alone together again. Whenever it was, it wouldn't be soon enough.

Chapter 20

The following Friday, after Heather finished getting dressed for work, she swung the kitchen door open with gusto and shuddered when she heard the loud thump.

"Argh!" Andrea yelped when the door struck her violently.

"Andie!" Heather exclaimed. She carefully opened the door and peered inside to see Andrea sitting on the kitchen floor holding her bloody head in her hands.

"Are you okay? I'm so sorry."

"I'm okay, it's just a scratch," Andrea insisted.

"It doesn't look like just a scratch. That's a lot of blood."

Heather crouched down next to Andrea, and pulled her hands away from her head to get a better look. The wound was over an inch long and it was bleeding profusely. She helped Andrea to her feet and over to a chair, careful not to get blood on her uniform.

She handed Andrea a wad of paper towels to use to apply pressure to the wound and went in search of a washcloth and first aid kit.

"Are you sure you're okay?" Heather asked when she returned. She gently washed the blood from Andrea's face and hands while Andrea maintained pressure on the gash.

"I'm fine. It doesn't even hurt." She lied. She felt a headache the size of Texas brewing and knew she was in for a long day.

"I think this needs stitches," Heather suggested, as she dabbed at it gently with the washcloth, trying to keep it from bleeding. "It's going to leave a scar."

"Some women might find that sexy," Andrea replied teasingly as she looked into Heather's concerned eyes.

"Do you?" Andrea asked.

Heather gasped when Andrea slipped her hand behind her neck and pulled her forward into a kiss. It was a hungry kiss and Heather struggled to sustain the contact as she straddled Andrea on the chair.

"It's about time," Heather whispered into the kiss.

Andrea's hands, of their own volition, began their quest for flesh. She released the buttons on Heather's navy blue blazer while her tongue teased Heather's lips, refusing to give in to the invitation to enter. She struggled with the buttons on Heather's white blouse and gave up. Needing more room to manoeuvre, she stood up, with Heather's legs wrapped around her waist, easily took ten paces across the room, and set her down on the countertop.

Heather was breathing heavily, nearly gasping. Her body was on fire. She couldn't get close enough to Andie. She fought to pull her closer, grasping desperately at any part of Andie she could reach.

Andrea unzipped Heather's pants to free the offending blouse. Her hands tingled when they finally made contact with the warm soft flesh of Heather's back. She moaned, pulled out of the kiss, and started to work on the top buttons of Heather's blouse. She took one look at Heather's flushed face, bruised lips, heavily lidded eyes, and ripped the blouse open, buttons landing loudly on the kitchen floor.

She kissed her way down Heather's neck and buried her face in the exposed cleavage. Heather could no longer participate. She was lost. Her head fell back in offering. Her hands fell to her sides, gripping the countertop to keep from slipping. Andrea deftly released the clasp of Heather's bra and freed her beautiful breasts from the confining garment.

Heather opened her eyes and caught sight of the clock on the wall.

"Shit, Andie, stop," she shouted while pushing Andrea away.

Andrea stepped back startled. She took in her surroundings and realized what she had done.

"I'm sorry, I shouldn't have ... I thought ..." Andrea started to say.

Heather pressed her finger to Andrea's lips to silence her.

"Shh! Give me your hand," Heather said before taking Andrea's hand and slipping it into her pants. She shuddered and whimpered at the contact.

"Hea ... ther," Andrea hissed.

"Do you feel that? How wet I am for you," Heather asked. "Don't apologize for anything but your lousy timing," she added before regrettably removing Andrea's hand from her pants. She gently pushed her away, slid off the countertop, and kissed her softly on the lips.

"I'm very late for work. And because of you, I have to shower again and try to find another clean uniform." She playfully shoved Andrea out of the way and left the kitchen, leaving a bewildered Andrea standing there alone.

"She wants me, she wants me," Andrea sang and did a happy dance. She slipped on one of the buttons on the floor and landed with a thud on her ass, laughing hysterically.

Twenty minutes later, Andrea walked Heather to the door. They stood shyly, looking anywhere but at each other. Finally, Andrea broke the silence.

"When will you be home?"

Heather met her eyes and said, "Tomorrow night, around seven. I wish I didn't have to go," she admitted and stepped closer to Andrea, nearly begging to be kissed again.

Andrea softly caressed her face and said, "I'll be counting the minutes." She leaned forward and kissed Heather tenderly.

Heather stepped back, took one last look at Andrea, stood up on her tiptoes to kiss the gash on her head, and walked out to her car. Andrea stood in the open doorway until Heather's car disappeared down the driveway.

She spent the rest of the day trying to plan a wonderfully romantic, candle lit dinner but realized that it would be useless. They'd end up in bed and skip dinner entirely. There was no way they'd be able to sit through dinner unless they went out, so she made a reservation at a nice romantic restaurant.

Time was passing too slowly—*only one thousand, two hundred and forty-two minutes to go*, she said to herself when she glanced at the clock on her nightstand. Sleep was coming in short spurts. She tossed and turned, unable to relax. The taste of Heather's flesh still lingered on her lips. Tomorrow night felt like it was a year away.

At some point, she dozed off and didn't wake again until her cell phone started ringing at eight in the morning.

"Reynolds," she answered cheerfully, thinking that maybe it was Heather calling.

"Andrea, it's Mr. Crowley. I'm sorry to disturb you on a Saturday morning, but I have a crisis in Mexico. I need you to get down there as soon as possible."

Not today, Andrea screamed without her voice.

"Is there anyone else who can go, sir?" she asked hopefully.

"They're very angry. I need your talent, Andrea. You're the only one who can make this better. Terri will be calling you with your flight information."

"Okay, sir. I'll be in touch," she replied, looked upward as if to ask God why this had to happen today, and got out of bed.

Terri called five minutes later.

"Your flight leaves in two and a half hours, Reynolds. You better hurry."

"You know, Terri, this could not have happened at a worse time. I had a special evening planned for Heather."

"Sorry, Reynolds. It's not my fault. I'm just doing my job," Terri said sympathetically.

"I know. I'm just so disappointed. Did anyone happen to tell you what the problem was?"

"Something about the parts cracking during installation," Terri replied.

Andrea felt defeated. This was not going to be just a quick overnight trip. She wouldn't be able to repair or retrofit the parts—she would have to wait for new parts to arrive. She would be there for days, maybe even weeks.

After getting her flight information from Terri, she began packing clothes and realized she might as well pack everything. It could be a while before she got back.

She spent a few minutes cleaning the gash on her forehead, which had started to bleed again from the exertion of packing. It did need stitches, but she could do nothing about that now. She applied a clean bandage that she hoped didn't look ridiculous, and took one last look around her now empty bedroom before closing the door.

She wrote out a long letter of apology to Heather, telling her she was sorry about the timing of this, and that she'd call her as soon as she could. She wasn't entirely happy with the letter she had written—it didn't convey what she was feeling. There was so much more she wanted to tell her, so much that she had planned on telling her that night at dinner, but she didn't have the time. She left the note on the table near the phone and rushed to the airport.

Heather couldn't believe she had to leave Andie to go to work. She'd been waiting most of her life for that moment and when it finally happened, she had to leave. She did her best to do her job well, but she couldn't keep her mind from drifting to Andie.

Even her co-workers were asking if she was okay. They asked if she was coming down with the flu or something. She was definitely coming down with something, and there was only one cure—a regular dose of Andie.

Andrea was greeted at the plant in Mexico by a mob of angry businessmen, who were managing to communicate their displeasure with her, despite their broken English. She followed them through the plant, and when she saw the parts, she realized with great disappointment, that there was no other solution. It would be days before she would see any replacement parts from Cinci-Plastics and it was clear that there would be no way to salvage any of the parts already there—every part in inventory was the same.

She did her best to assure them that the situation would be handled quickly and effectively, but she knew they didn't care. They wanted their problem fixed today. She began preparing herself for the onslot of scrutiny and condemnation she'd receive over the next few days, until the parts arrived. She'd have to sit there every day with nothing to do but wait. It would be torture. She'd have nothing better to do than think of Heather, which would only make the days last longer.

CHAPTER 21

Rebecca walked into the house, surprised to find it empty. She was packing up a box of books and CD's in the living room when she noticed a note by the phone. Intrigued, she walked over and read it. Sensing an opportunity to win Heather back, she crumpled the note, threw it in the trash, and waited for Heather to come home.

"What are you doing here?" Heather asked when Rebecca greeted her at the door.

"I came to pick up the rest of my stuff," Rebecca said innocently.

"Where's Andie?" Heather asked curiously. She had expected to come home to find Andie anxiously waiting for her; instead, it was Rebecca.

"Gone," Rebecca replied.

"Gone where?"

"I don't know, but her room is empty," Rebecca said. She had taken the liberty of checking Andrea's room and hiding any of the little things she had left behind.

Heather ran to Andie's bedroom in disbelief. Her heart sank when she realized it was empty. She ran for the phone and dialed Andie's cell phone number. The message she received was that the customer she was trying to reach was unavailable. This couldn't be happening again. Andie couldn't have just left again without saying anything. She wouldn't do that ... would she?

Heather began to sob. She rushed into her own bedroom, hurled herself on the bed, and cried like she had never cried before.

The phone rang and Rebecca answered it quickly.

"Hello," she said politely.

"Rebecca? Is Heather home?" Andrea thought it odd that Rebecca was answering the phone.

"No, she's not," Rebecca said coolly.

Andrea thought she heard something sinister in the tone of Rebecca's voice but disregarded it quickly.

"What are you doing there?"

"Just picking up some of my things."

Andrea asked Rebecca to write down the phone number for her hotel and asked her to have Heather call her and let her know that for some reason her cell phone wasn't working.

Rebecca had enough sense to write the number down so she could repeat it to Andrea, but as soon as she hung up, she through it in the trash.

"Who was on the phone?" Heather asked, hoping that it may have been Andie, when she emerged from her room a few minutes later dressed in an old pair of sweats.

"Wrong number," Rebecca replied glumly.

"Oh!" Heather said dejectedly as she threw herself on the couch.

Rebecca approached her slowly and caressed her tear-stained face.

"Are you okay?"

Heather shook her head no and allowed herself to accept all of the comfort Rebecca was willing to give her that night.

Heather was in the shower and Rebecca was lying on the bed the next morning with a smug look on her face when the phone rang again.

"Hello," Rebecca said blissfully.

"Why are you there again, Rebecca," Andrea asked anxiously.

"Just came back to pick up a few more things," she said innocently.

"Is Heather home?"

Rebecca walked closer to the bathroom door so that Andrea would hear the water running and said, "She's in the shower. I gave her your message. I'm sure she'll call you when she gets a chance," she added almost defiantly.

Andrea was sure she heard the shower running, which meant Rebecca was in Heather's room with her. That thought caused a flash of jealousy to shoot through her.

"Okay, just tell her I called again," she said lamely. She had her suspicions about what was going on, but was helpless to do anything from so far away, especially when she couldn't even get Heather on the phone.

Rebecca was glad Heather hadn't heard the phone ring that time so she wouldn't have to lie to her again about who it was. When Heather greeted her with a pained expression on her face, she almost felt guilty for taking advantage of her—almost, but not really. She had what she wanted, and that was Heather. By the time Andrea returned, Heather would have forgotten all about her, or they'd hate each other ... *even better*, she decided.

Rebecca looked compassionately into Heather's sad eyes before crossing the room to take her in her arms.

"How are you feeling this morning," she asked sincerely. Although Heather hadn't rebuffed her advances the previous night, she knew that her mind had been elsewhere. That made this whole game just a little more entertaining. Heather was undoubtedly feeling guilty about what happened.

Feeling? Heather thought to herself. *I feel like someone ripped my chest open, tore out my heart, and stepped on it.*

"Pretty good," she lied.

"You know what you need?" Rebecca suggested. "You need to get out of this house for a while. Why don't we go do something fun?"

"I don't really feel like it," Heather replied.

"Sure you do. You just have to get through the door, and then you'll feel better," Rebecca assured. She was desperate to get Heather out of the house and away from the phone and the memories of Andrea.

"Fine," Heather answered. She didn't have the energy to argue.

"Where are we going?" Heather asked as they drove down the highway in Rebecca's car.

"You'll see when we get there. It's a surprise," Rebecca replied mysteriously.

The final twenty minutes of the trip were made in silence. When Rebecca slowed at the entrance to Tanglewood, Heather nearly burst into tears.

Under different circumstances, the holiday light display would have been magical. All it did now was remind Heather of how much fun she and Andie used to have during the holidays. How ironic was it that she was planning to bring Andie to Tanglewood Christmas Eve? Andie would have been impressed by the magnificent display. It was quite remarkable in comparison to those they had seen growing up. Her mind drifted to their daily routine of holiday light viewing.

By the time Andrea would finish her chores at home, it was already dark outside so she'd rush over to pick Heather up and away they'd go. Every day, they went to a dif-

ferent part of town. They'd make a map of the best houses and make plans to visit them again closer to Christmas.

The Parker house was one of those houses. The house itself was nothing special; it was a bit rundown to be honest, but come the Christmas season, it was outstanding. On the roof, there was a life-size sleigh with reindeer, and a Santa balancing precariously on the edge of the chimney. How he wasn't blown down with the strong winds, they never knew, but he was impressive. The sleigh was made of wood and steel. Even the reindeer where covered in fake fur to make them look authentic. No cheap plastic decorations at the Parker house.

The lawn display was equally impressive. There was a large ice rink, which covered more than half of the yard. Several elves dressed in red and green somehow skated around the rink. How the elves could skate around and not bump into each other was another mystery. They asked several people, but no one ever knew. Heather wondered if the Parker house still existed.

Heather had been so caught up in her memories of Andie and the Parker house that she hadn't noticed Rebecca pulling off to the side of the path that led through the park.

"What are you thinking about?" Rebecca asked.

"Nothing. Why did you pull over?"

"I don't know. It's kind of romantic out here, don't you think? All these beautiful lights. There's no one else around. I just thought we could enjoy it for a couple of minutes," she said as she removed her seat belt and scooted across the front seat to be at Heather's side.

Heather prayed that if she shut her eyes, Andie would be the one sitting next to her when she opened them. But Andie was gone. She had hurt her again—and even worse, she had done it the same way.

Beside herself with grief, she melted into Rebecca's embrace and didn't struggle when Rebecca kissed her. Consumed by the passion derived from her pain, she kissed her back and pulled her closer. When Rebecca slipped her hand beneath her shirt to cup her breast, Heather was shocked back into reality.

"Stop," she said breathlessly. "Please take me home."

Why was she feeling guilty? She had no reason to feel guilty. Andie did the unthinkable, so why not fall back into Rebecca's loving arms if she'd take her. At least she wouldn't be alone this time while she tried to get over Andie. If nothing else, Rebecca would be good company.

Two days later, Andrea's imagination was getting the better of her after not hearing from Heather yet. Heather not calling just wasn't sitting right with her—it wasn't like Heather not to return her calls. Something was definitely wrong. She kept having visions of Heather in Rebecca's arms. It was driving her crazy.

To make matters worse, things at the plant weren't going well. There was nothing she could do to fix the problem until the replacement parts arrived. She felt lost and alone and just wanted to hear Heather's voice. She decided to try to call her again, hoping she might reach her this time. When the answering machine picked up, the greeting she heard shattered whatever hope she had left that she would ever be with Heather.

"Hi, you've reached Heather and Rebecca. We're not in right now. Please leave a message after the beep and we'll call you back."

That was not the greeting that was on the answering machine when Andrea left for Mexico. It was a new greeting, and in Rebecca's voice. Consumed with rage she slammed the phone receiver into its cradle, threw herself on the bed, and screamed into her pillow. How could Heather do this to her? Why? She said she didn't love Rebecca. Why did she lie?

Startled out of her tantrum by the ringing telephone, she gathered her composure, thinking for an instant that it might be Heather, and answered it.

Her glimmer of hope faded when the person on the other end of the line informed her that the replacement parts from Cinci-Plastics had arrived at the plant. She pushed aside her grief, dragged herself off the bed, and headed to the plant.

She quickly took care of removing the defective parts and replacing them with the new ones. At eleven in the morning, her work there was done and she was going to be able to go home much sooner then she had originally anticipated. But what was she going home to? She tried to ignore the facts, but couldn't. They were laid out before her in giant neon lights. Heather and Rebecca were back together. She made one final attempt at calling Heather. The answering machine picked up and she took several deep breaths to steady herself when she was greeted with Rebecca's voice.

"Hey, Heather, just wanted to let you know I'm on my way back. I'll be home sometime tonight," she managed, though her voice cracked with pain as she spoke.

Rebecca listened to the phone message, laughed, hit the delete button, and tried to come up with a plan to keep Heather from being home when Andrea arrived. One more night—that's all she wanted. She decided to invite Heather to dinner at her apartment for a change and then convince her to spend the night. She was surprised at how easily Heather agreed. She knew then, that she had won.

Exhausted and defeated, Andrea walked into the quiet house and looked around for clues to help confirm or refute her suspicions. Nothing seemed out of place, but Rebecca had definitely brought back most of her belongings, if she had even moved any out in the first place.

Despondently, she walked to her room and began unpacking her clothes even though she knew she wouldn't be able to stay there now that Heather had made her feelings known.

How could Heather have gone back to Rebecca? There was no denying what happened that afternoon in the kitchen before she left. Heather had wanted her. Was it all just a plot for revenge? Had Heather been secretly harbouring her anger? Had she been planning this the whole time? Had she been waiting for the perfect opportunity, when Andrea was at her most vulnerable to strike back?

Andrea knew it was wrong to go into Heather's room, but she had to know for sure. When she saw Rebecca's dirty clothes scattered on the floor, there was no doubt. The bed had been slept in by more than one person.

How could you do this to me, Heather? she asked the empty room.

Solemnly, she walked back to her own room and cried herself to sleep.

Chapter 22

▼

Andrea woke to the sound of voices in the living room. She glanced at the clock. It was seven in the morning. How she managed to sleep through the night, she didn't know.

Time to face reality, she thought to herself as she rolled out of bed and threw some clothes over her body.

The anger in Heather's eyes when they met hers could only be matched by the fear in Rebecca's.

"I've got to go," Rebecca said quickly before escaping through the front door. She knew they would be furious with her once they figured out what she had done. That didn't matter. She had managed to accomplish her goal. Heather and Andrea hated each other, and she was rewarded with a few extra nights in bed with Heather for her efforts. She had won.

Andrea and Heather stood silently, glaring at each other. Andrea was so angry and hurt, that she was shaking.

"Why, Heather?" she asked.

"Why?" Heather screamed. "After what you did, you want to know why? I can't believe you. How could you do that to me again?"

Andrea had no idea what Heather was talking about.

"What did I do?" she asked innocently.

"Don't play innocent with me," Heather raged. "You have a lot of nerve coming back here after what you did."

"What did I do?" she asked again.

"You know damn well what you did."

"I honestly don't," Andrea pleaded. "You're the one who didn't call me back. How could you get back together with Rebecca after …?"

Heather interrupted, "How could I call you back? Wait! You called?"

"Yes, I called. I also left a note. Rebecca told me she gave you the messages."

"Oh my God! I'm going to be sick!" Heather said as she shoved Andrea out of the way and made it to her bathroom just in time to empty the contents of her stomach.

After a few minutes, Andrea quietly slipped into Heather's bathroom and prepared a cool washcloth for her.

"I'm such a fool," Heather said through her sobs. "She never gave me the messages, Andie. I should have known she would do something like this."

"You slept with her," Andrea stated as more of a question.

Heather met her eyes. Andrea could see the shame. She didn't need to hear the answer. She stood and left the room.

Andrea sat on her bed for a long time trying to understand. She couldn't for the life of her, fathom any excuse to justify Heather's sleeping with Rebecca. She packed her bags and checked into a hotel near the plant.

Heather cried for what seemed like hours. How could she have thought Andie would hurt her again? How could she have been so vulnerable that she became a puppet in Rebecca's manipulative game of revenge?

For a few minutes, rage was a welcome relief for the grief, and she stormed around the house, picked up anything that belonged to Rebecca, and chucked it out the door. The sounds of Rebecca's most precious possessions shattering on the concrete floor two storeys below were almost therapeutic. When there was nothing left to throw, she began to cry again. She hated Rebecca. She hated herself more for allowing Rebecca to deceive her.

Three days had passed and Heather had not left her room. From somewhere deep in her soul, she found the courage to dial Andrea's number. She expected to get her voicemail, and she had rehearsed the message she was going to leave several times. When Andrea answered the phone, she lost her ability to speak.

"Reynolds," Andrea said in her usual greeting, without checking first to see who was calling.

After several long moments of silence, she looked down at her phone and recognized Heather's phone number.

"Heather?" she said softly. The last three days had been pure hell. She was torn between her disappointment in Heather, and her never-ending love for the woman. The least she could do was let her explain.

"Andie," Heather started shakily. "I expected to get your voicemail ..." She lost her voice, choking back the tears.

Andrea ached for her. She shared the pain she heard in Heather's voice.

"Would you rather call back and leave me a message?" she offered.

"No," Heather replied and took several deep breaths to calm herself. "Do you have time to meet me somewhere ... so we can talk?"

It was Andrea's turn to be silent. She yearned to see Heather again, despite the pain. It was too soon though. She needed more time.

"Not really," she lied as she stared blankly into the television set in her hotel room. "I'll give you a call when I get some free time," she said and quickly hung up before completely losing her ability to speak.

Heather waited by the phone for days, afraid if she left that she'd miss Andie's call. After a week, she gave up hope. Andie wasn't going to call her. She had to get herself together. Sitting by the phone wasn't paying the mountain of bills that were beginning to accumulate. Going back to work would help, but even if she took all of the available hours, she would never be able to manage on her own. She'd have to sell the house. Maybe that wasn't such a bad thing. That house contained a lot of memories.

Memories of Donna were everywhere. Her bedroom reminded her of Rebecca, and if she dared go in the kitchen, all she could think of was Andie. Andie's lips. Andie's hands.

She screamed at the top of her lungs. It was a loud, primal scream full of anguish, which left her throat raw. Strangely enough, she felt a bit better afterwards. After calling to schedule an appointment with her real estate agent, she called her boss to say she was ready to go back to work.

Day by day, it got a little bit easier, but still, she cried herself to sleep every night. On the Saturday before Christmas, Heather decided to brave the mall. She hadn't even started her shopping yet. Christmas had always been a special time for her growing up. Christmas Eve was a night she'd especially look forward to because Andie would be with her. Andie never missed Christmas Eve.

Her mother would prepare a lavish feast—turkey and all the fixings. The ham was saved for Christmas Day. Dinner would be on the table at exactly five o'clock.

One year, when Andie didn't show up on time for dinner, Heather was concerned. Even her parents seemed a little bit worried. It wasn't like Andie to miss a meal. They waited an hour and she still hadn't arrived.

"I know Andrea's not here yet, but we have to eat now or we'll be late for church," her mother said gently, trying not to let her concern show.

They ate in uncomfortable silence—each of them coming up with their own sordid story about what happened to Andrea.

After dinner, Heather stared out her window anxiously watching for Andie to arrive. She was dressed in a beautiful, flowing, green gown her mother had bought for her to wear to church. She heard the doorbell ring, but thought nothing of it—Andie wouldn't ring the doorbell, she'd crawl up through her window. But it was Andie—a broken, battered Andie. Her right arm was in a cast and she had a black eye.

"I apologize for being late. I hope you didn't wait for me," she was saying to Heather's parents.

As if sensing Heather's presence, she turned her attention from Mrs. Johnson to the stairs, where Heather stood, looking more beautiful than she had ever seen her. "Heather, you look amazing," she said in awe, hoping her true feelings didn't show.

Heather ran down the stairs and wanted to hold Andie in her arms, but stood a few feet away, afraid of hurting her.

"What happened?"

"I was up on the ladder, trying to fix a string of lights that had burnt out and I fell," Andrea said believably. It was the same story she had told at the hospital. The doctors found it believable, but Andrea could tell Heather wasn't buying it.

As the four of them walked to church, Heather slowed so that she and Andrea were walking several paces behind her parents.

"Your dad did that to you, didn't he?" she whispered.

Andrea didn't answer the question. She didn't have to. Heather knew her too well. She also knew that Andrea's family didn't put up Christmas lights.

"It's okay, Heather. I'm all right. I'll be better than ever, before you know it."

Heather couldn't believe how brave Andrea seemed that day. When they crawled into her tiny single bed that night, it was all Heather could do to stay on her own side. She wanted to hold Andie and protect her. That night she knew for sure her feelings for Andie were more than just friendly. Although she didn't really understand it, she knew she was in love with her.

Heather managed a façade of joy as she walked from store to store, looking for the perfect gifts for her co-workers. She had taken care of her parents by arranging a weeklong getaway for them in Hawaii over the holidays. Unfortunately, she had arranged their trip when she thought she'd be spending Christmas with Andie; now, she'd be spending it alone—she wasn't sure she'd survive.

On her way out of the mall, try as she might, she couldn't resist the urge to buy a shirt for Andie that caught her eye. She would look stunning in it. She tried to reason with herself, telling herself she wouldn't see her again, but she bought it anyway. If she didn't see her, maybe she could send it to her.

Chapter 23

Every night, Andrea stared at the phone and wrestled with the idea of calling Heather, and every night, she convinced herself that it was still too soon. With Christmas fast approaching, Andrea felt the way she had before she met Heather and her family. She felt alone and scared. The assembly plant would shutdown tomorrow for several days leaving Andrea with nothing to do but sit in her lonely hotel room.

Even Tammy and Jamie were gone for the holidays. She was happy for them though. Happy that they found what they needed in each other. When Tammy asked her to keep an eye on Mr. Snickers for them while they went away, she didn't hesitate to say yes. Despite their initial awkward and unpleasant greeting, Andrea and Mr. Snickers had become allies. That could have something to do with the fact that Andrea never failed to sneak treats to Mr. Snickers when she visited.

At least taking care of him made her feel needed. Oh, the patience he had. Each day, when she'd stop by to feed him, she'd tell him the sordid tales of her life. Despite his indifferent expression, she knew he somehow understood what she was saying. He was a wonderful listener. He'd sit on her lap for hours as she went on and on about Heather. When she'd cry, he'd stand up on his hind legs and lick her tears away.

Two days before Christmas, Andrea still hadn't started her shopping. She wasn't up to facing the festive crowds. For a few years, when she started celebrating Christmas with Heather and her family, it became her favourite holiday. For those few years, Andrea had felt all of the awe and wonder of a child at Christmas.

The Johnson's tree was something of a masterpiece. It was a holiday tradition that they would set out exactly two weeks before Christmas to cut down their own tree. Andrea loved making that trip with them. One year, they even let her choose the tree—it was an honour.

It had to be precisely nine feet tall when trimmed, have no less than two thousand lights, and each and every ornament had to be placed in a specific location according to a sketch they made. Every year, one new ornament was added and it always came with a story about where it came from (usually some distant land far away) or why it was purchased (because it reminded them of a particular place or person that they held dear). Andrea loved listening to their stories. It was her way of escaping her own terrible life.

Her own parents quit putting up a tree when she was ten. Her mother usually worked a double shift on Christmas day, so the holiday became just another day for Andrea, until she started celebrating with the Johnsons.

Andrea hadn't celebrated Christmas in eight years. She tried to tell herself that it didn't matter, that she didn't care—but she did. She had been so excited about spending Christmas with Heather this year; now, she just didn't care. Once again, it was just another day. Unfortunately, she'd have to suffer the warm and friendly holiday cheer while she braved the mall to pick up a few gifts.

First on her list was Carlos. He was a very proud man and a very frugal man. Despite the fact that he earned a very comfortable salary, he wouldn't spend any money on himself. He was always sending money home to his family. Always making sure his own children had the best of everything. A few weeks ago, Andrea noticed that Carlos had been using duct tape to hold together his dilapidated briefcase. She found a beautiful briefcase, that looked similar to what she thought his old one would have looked like when new, and bought it.

Shopping for Tammy and Jamie was more difficult. She wanted to get them something personal, but for them as a couple. The problem was that they were so different from one another she found it difficult to find something they'd both enjoy. During the course of her search, she kept finding things that Heather would like. Several times, she forgot, picked up the item, and was standing in the checkout line before she remembered that she wouldn't be seeing Heather this Christmas.

After two hours of searching, she settled on a painting by a local artist of a woman staring off into space, longing for something or someone. Her expression mirrored that of Tammy's when she used to look at Jamie. Hopefully, Tammy would recognize the expression and remember the feeling so that she would never take Jamie for granted. Jamie, on the other hand, would never understand the significance of the emotion. She would, however, enjoy looking at the beautiful woman.

She stopped at the jewellers and bought a lovely pair of diamond earrings for Terri. On her way home, she would stop and have them over-nighted to her. She wished she had called Terri to see what her plans were. At least they could have kept each other company. Knowing Terri though, she probably had plenty of company anyway.

Andrea cringed when she saw the watch display. Mindlessly, she selected two that Heather would like, but she didn't buy them; instead, she rushed to the pet store to shop for Mr. Snickers.

She was undecided about what to get for him, since he was already very spoiled and had everything a cat could want. When she spied the giant cat tree, she fretted over how she would get it home, but immediately knew he had to have it. After spending fifteen minutes wrestling it into her SUV, she finally made it fit. It would stay there until she was ready to give it to him on Christmas morning, if she was able to get it out of the SUV at all.

"Merry Christmas, Mr. Snickers," she said to the adorable feline when she arrived to feed him on Christmas morning dragging the giant cat tree behind her.

He looked at her almost sympathetically, but was quickly enthralled with his new gift. He spent several hours playing in that tree and Andrea did all that she could to coax him out of it. She was lonely and wanted to cuddle him, but he was a cat and did as he pleased.

"No offence, Mr. Snickers, but sometimes I wish you were a dog," she said as she reached for the remote and began surfing the channels for something to occupy her mind.

Why she decided to stop on *It's A Wonderful Life*, she didn't know. By the time it was over, she was sobbing uncontrollably. Mr. Snickers suddenly appeared by her side, and then strutted to the front door, as if asking her to follow him.

"What is it, Mr. Snickers?"

When she didn't follow, he returned to her side, and then walked to the door again.

"What do you need? You know you can't go out that door." He was back at her side again and began pushing her with his head.

"What are you trying to tell me?" she asked in frustration.

He coaxed her to the door, and then began pacing back in forth.

"I don't understand what you're telling me."

Without warning, he made a sound so strange, she was sure she had misheard.

"Did you just say Heather?" It couldn't be. She must be losing her mind. Had Mr. Snickers been a dog, she might have believed it, but he wasn't. Cat's only meowed and purred. They couldn't make other sounds, could they? She looked at him in disbelief and he made the sound again. Clearly two syllables—two syllables that sounded an awful lot like Heather. Maybe she thought that's what she heard, because deep down, that's what she wanted to hear.

He was trying to tell her what she already knew to be true; no matter what Heather had done, she couldn't live without her one minute longer.

She said goodbye to Mr. Snickers and rushed back over to the hotel to take a shower and change her clothes.

On the way to Heather's she realized that she probably wouldn't be home alone on Christmas Day. Heather probably went to Florida to visit her parents, or worse yet, maybe she was with Rebecca. To her relief, Heather's car was in the driveway.

Andrea's stomach was in knots by the time she reached the top of the stairs. She knocked softly and waited. There was no answer. She knocked again. Still nothing. She tried to listen through the door, but she couldn't hear anything. Disappointed and discouraged, she made her way back down the stairs, where she caught the faint glimpse of something moving around in the woods behind the house.

With a great deal of difficulty, she was able to discern that it was Heather. She sat on the stairs and waited for what seemed like an eternity, for Heather to materialize in front of her. She stood nervously and kicked shyly at a pebble by her foot, unable to look at Heather's tear-stained face. Finally, she looked up.

"Merry Christmas, Heather," she said softly and opened her arms in invitation.

"Oh, Andie!" Heather replied and jumped into Andrea's arms.

Andrea struggled to catch her breath. Heather was squeezing her so tightly that she was choking her.

"Heather," she said raggedly. "I can't breathe."

Heather let her go and backed up a couple of paces. She looked into Andie's gorgeous face and begged for forgiveness.

"Andie, I'm so sorry. I made a terrible mistake. Please ..."

"Heather, don't. Just don't okay," Andrea said dismissively. She didn't want to hear explanations. She knew in her heart that whatever Heather's reasoning was, it wouldn't take away the disappointment. She wanted Heather, but she wanted to let go of the past. All of it.

Heather had started to cry again and Andie pulled her close.

"Don't try to explain, Heather. It won't change what happened."

"That's it then? There's no room for discussion. It's over." Heather shivered though she didn't know if it was because of the cold, or because of the reality of the words she had said.

"You're cold, Heather. Let's go inside and talk," Andrea suggested.

"What point is there in talking if you aren't willing to listen?" Heather said coolly. Why did Andie come back, if she wasn't willing to listen? Why was she torturing her, especially on Christmas Day?

Andrea leaned forward and captured Heather's lips softly with her own.

"That's the point," she said. "Now, let's go upstairs and talk."

A dazed and confused Heather followed Andrea up the stairs, into the house and to the kitchen. She sat silently at the table, wondering what Andie was thinking, why she had come back, and why she had kissed her.

Andrea said nothing as she made them each a cup of hot chocolate before sitting down across from Heather at the table.

"Heather, I've done a lot of thinking. Actually, I've done nothing but think since the day I left," Andrea admitted.

"I was wondering if we could start over ... forget about the mistakes we've *both* made ... forget about everything and just start fresh."

Heather sat for a few seconds contemplating Andrea's offer. She didn't care what she had to do, as long as she could be with her.

She smiled and said, "Hi, I'm Heather. It's a pleasure to meet you."

Andrea stood, pulling Heather up with her and said, "I'm Andie." She allowed a mischievous grin to appear on her lips as she lifted Heather off the ground and into her arms. "Would you like to see my bed—it's really quite impressive."

"Sounds intriguing," Heather replied seductively.

"Andie, please don't drop me ... the way things have been going so far ... it would be just our luck," she said seriously.

"I'll never drop you, Heather. But I can't promise I won't bang your head off the door jamb on the way into the bedroom."

Heather's eyes widened with fear and she tried to get Andrea to put her down.

"Relax," Andrea said, "I was only joking."

Chapter 24

Andrea hovered over Heather's body, consciously avoiding contact. Their bodies separated by merely inches, but feeling like miles. She lowered her head just enough to allow her lips to softly capture Heather's. The sensation was incredible. Since their lips were the only point of contact, the kiss was felt through their entire bodies. Andrea trembled, her arms starting to give way. She wanted to prolong the amazing sensation, but knew her arms would betray her soon. She teased Heather's lower lip with her tongue, requesting entry into the hot, wet recess of her mouth.

Heather obliged, her hungry mouth wanting all of Andie. She pulled Andie to her, seeking contact. When their bodies finally converged, Andie moaned and pulled away from the kiss.

Andrea softly whispered, "I love you, Heather," into her ear before kissing her way down Heather's neck and back up to her lips. She could kiss Heather forever and never tire of it, but Heather had other ideas. She began tugging desperately at Andrea's shirt in an effort to remove it.

Andrea pulled away and smiled mischievously. She was not going to let Heather rush her. She had waited nearly her entire life for this moment and she was going to make it last as long as she could. She reached for Heather's right hand with her left one and laced their fingers together before slithering down so that her head was resting on Heather's hip. With her free hand, she gently pushed Heather's light pink t-shirt up ever so slightly, baring her smooth flat stomach. She trailed soft, wet kisses along the sensitive flesh and slowly slid Heather's shirt up, exposing her delicate, velvety skin, inch-by-inch, stopping just short of her beautiful breasts.

With her thumb, she gently caressed the underside of Heather's breast through the thin silky fabric of her bra. Heather moaned and arched into Andie, seeking more contact.

"God, Andie! I knew it would be like this with you," she said through ragged breaths. Her voice deep and raspy with desire.

Andrea met her eyes questioningly and asked, "Like what?"

"Soft … slow … passionate … sensual …" Heather started to say but Andrea gently stroked her nipple and she lost her voice.

"Are those good things?" Andrea asked seductively as she teased Heather's still bra-covered nipple with her teeth.

Heather struggled to answer. Her heavy short breaths making speech difficult.

"All but the slow part. I can't take it. If you don't touch me soon, I'm going to spontaneously combust."

"No you won't; besides, we've waited this long, what's a couple more hours?"

Heather was horrified. "Hours, Andie?"

"Well, at least one. You're not even naked yet," Andrea insisted.

"There is a simple solution to that problem, you know." Heather was certain she wouldn't last another ten minutes, let alone an hour or more.

Andrea ignored her suggestion and continued the deliberately slow exploration of the body she'd dreamed of most of her life.

"Will you at least let me touch you, Andie? Take your shirt off. Please!" She didn't wait for a reply. She quickly began to unbutton her shirt, the minute Andrea shifted to give her access. Her strategy was to get Andrea so excited that she would have to speed things up a little bit.

Andrea wore only a thin tank top under her button-down denim shirt allowing her darker, coffee coloured areolas to appear beneath the nearly transparent fabric. She teased Andrea's nipples through the fabric and it appeared as though her strategy was paying off until she heard Andie whimper, felt her shudder and let out long relaxing breath. Heather didn't know whether to be amazed or disappointed. She gave Andie a few minutes of uninterrupted exploration to recover before returning her attention to her beautiful, but clearly oversensitive nipples.

Andrea pulled away and finally got down to business, or so Heather thought, when she unbuttoned her jeans and removed them. Oh, how wrong she was.

"Andie, please touch me," she pleaded again when Andie began caressing her ankles.

This time, Andrea met her desperate gaze and her resolve faded away. She peeled off her tank top and kicked free of her jeans in seconds before returning her attention to Heather's still-covered breasts.

"You're gorgeous," Heather whispered.

"Your eyes are closed," Andrea replied.

"I know what you look like. Your naked body is forever seared in my mind."

"As is yours in mine," Andrea said as she pulled Heather to a sitting position, gently removed her t-shirt, and slipped the bra from her shoulders.

"Beautiful," she said with awe before capturing Heather's nipple with her lips and lowering her back down on the bed.

Heather heard Andrea whimper again, felt the now-familiar trembling and was not the least bit shocked when the result of Andrea's orgasm coated her thigh.

"I'm sorry. It's just that … I've waited so long for this day, and you're so beautiful. I lose myself with you," Andrea said bashfully.

"Don't apologize, Andie. I think it's beautiful, the way you love me," Heather replied reassuringly. "But I do believe the score is two to nothing though, so could you maybe speed things up a little so I can catch up?"

"Tell me what you need."

"Do whatever you want, Andie. Just do it faster," Heather pleaded.

Andrea kissed her passionately, one hand caressing her face, while the other explored the sensitive flesh of Heather's inner thighs. She slipped her finger into the wet, welcoming folds and moaned into Heather's mouth.

"You're so wet," Andrea exclaimed.

"Only for you, Andie."

Heather lifted her hips to enhance the contact of Andrea's painfully slow, featherlike strokes.

"I need you inside me, Andie," Heather said urgently.

"I love you," Andrea said softly before slipping inside her.

She felt Heather tighten around her fingers as she slipped in deeper. Heather's hips rocked urgently against her hand. Heather's soft cries as her orgasm approached were Andrea's final undoing. She struggled to keep up with Heather's frantic writhing as her own powerful orgasm shook through her body.

"I love you," Heather whispered into Andie's ear just before her body arched wildly, shook violently, then collapsed limply on the bed beneath Andrea.

When she was able to move again, Andrea gently rolled onto her side and looked with awe at Heather's beauty.

"Wow," Heather said quietly. She would have said something more profound, but speaking took more energy than she had at the moment.

Andrea smiled and gently stroked her hair. The innocent contact shot a sudden bolt of arousal through Heather and instantly energized her lifeless body. She rolled over and pinned Andrea to the bed.

"Heather, I can't yet. That last one did me in for a while, I think," Andrea admitted while trying to wiggle away from Heather's exploring hands.

"Hush," Heather said and planted a soft kiss on Andrea's lips, "I'll go slow."

"Hi," Andrea said lazily after opening her eyes to find Heather lying next to her wide-awake. She shyly pulled a thin sheet over her naked body. Shyly? How could she be shy in Heather's presence after the things they'd done to each other the night before, and again, just a couple of hours ago? Maybe it was the uneasy way Heather was looking at her. Almost as if, last night had been a mistake.

"How long have you been awake?" Andrea asked softly.

"About an hour," Heather replied.

"Why didn't you wake me?" Andrea asked. She had only slept a couple of hours but still, she felt more rested and relaxed than she ever had.

"I was watching you sleep ... and thinking."

"Talk to me, Heather. Do you regret what happened?" She knew in her heart, that she would die if Heather had any regrets.

"Regret? No. That's not the right word." Heather sighed. Her concerns rested with what Andie was thinking. What was last night to her? Was that all she wanted from her? Just the one night of passion that eluded them as teenagers. She wanted so badly for it to be more, but she sensed that Andie was holding back.

"What is the *right* word then?" Andrea asked with great concern, now propped up on her elbow so she could see the expression on Heather's face.

"I don't know, Andie," she said with frustration. "What was last night to you?"

"Last night was the most amazing night of my life."

"But what did it mean to you?"

"It meant the world to me. You made all my dreams come true."

"And now?"

"And now, what?" Andrea's frustration was mounting. She couldn't for the life of her understand what it was Heather was trying to ask.

"Was this it for us? Was that all you wanted from me?" She didn't want to let her insecurities show, but she couldn't hide the tears which flowed freely from her eyes.

"Heather, you know I love you. I'm in love with you. I don't ever want to let you go again."

"Andie, I need more than this. I need all of you. Not just the parts you are willing to share. I need the parts of you that you keep hidden from the rest of the world. If you can't share that with me, this is all we can ever have."

"Heather," Andrea whispered as she wiped the tears from Heather's cheek. "I want to give you all of me."

Andrea gathered Heather in her arms and held her close. She felt the walls she had carefully erected come crumbling down inside her. That moment, she became a completely different person.

Heather watched this transformation in awe. Andie's eyes, which were more often than not, expressionless, now bared her soul. Emotions never exposed before, flooded those expressive eyes. The pain, the fear, and more than anything, the love she felt for Heather.

Andrea made love to her so passionately, so completely, that the final shreds of doubt that Heather had were washed away as if they never existed. She gave Heather all of her. Then they wept. Wept for the time they lost, the joy they felt, the pain they now shared. They became one in mind, body, and soul.

When they woke later that afternoon, Andrea looked around her bedroom and realized that everything she owned was still at the hotel.

"Heather, I have to go out for a little while to pick up my stuff. I don't even have a clean shirt to wear."

"Wait, I almost forgot," Heather said before springing from the bed and rushing out of the room.

When she returned a few minutes later, she had a box wrapped in fancy foil Christmas paper. She crawled back into bed next to Andie and handed her the box.

"You bought me something?" Andrea asked, feeling guilty for ignoring her impulse to buy Heather something for Christmas.

"It's no big deal, Andie. It's just something I saw that I knew you had to have. I honestly didn't think I'd get to give it to you in person. I was going to send it to the hotel."

"I feel bad that I didn't get you anything. I almost did, but I put it back. Coming here yesterday wasn't something I planned. Something inside me just snapped and I drove over here not really knowing what to expect," Andrea admitted.

"You didn't have to get me anything; besides, you being here is the best gift I could ever ask for." She kissed Andrea lightly on the lips. "Open it already."

Andrea quickly opened the box.

"I guess I have a clean shirt after all," Andrea said as she lifted the blue-grey shirt from the box and held it up in front of her.

"I love it. Thank you. But shirt or no shirt, I still have to go out," she said softly before taking Heather into her arms.

"I don't want to let you go," Heather whined. "Not now, not ever again."

Suddenly, it dawned on her that Andrea's work required her to be away from home for long periods of time.

"How am I going to survive when you're working for weeks on end in some other part of the country?"

Andrea sensed Heather's anxiety over this and knew what she had to do. She knew that the position Carlos tried to get her to take a couple of months ago had still not been filled.

"Let's say, just for argument's sake, that I didn't have to travel ... would you still want to live in this house. Do you like living here?"

"I love this house, Andie. If you don't, we can move, but I really love it. The only reason I put it up for sale was because I couldn't afford it on my own. What do you mean you might not have to travel?"

"Don't you worry about it. I have a plan. I'll be home in a few hours," she said before getting out of bed.

"God, you're gorgeous," Heather said at the sight of Andrea's naked body. After spending nearly twenty-four hours with that naked body, she was amazed that she still found it so overwhelming.

"Andie, don't take this the wrong way, but your plans often have disastrous results."

"Not this one," Andrea assured her before escaping to the shower. "Get some rest while I'm gone, you'll need it."

Chapter 25

▼

Once Andrea was gone, Heather took a quick shower and began moving her things from her bedroom to Andrea's. She didn't want to be reminded of Rebecca. Unfortunately, even though her room was a bit bigger, just being in it, reminded her of Rebecca and what she'd done. Maybe it was a bit presumptuous on her part to assume Andrea wouldn't mind, but it felt like the right thing to do. She didn't realize how much stuff she had until she sat in the center of Andrea's room and looked around. She had clothes piled everywhere.

It had taken her nearly three hours to move everything. She was exhausted. Hopefully Andie wouldn't be upset. It was too late to worry about it now; it was done. Andie would be home any time now and there was no way she'd have the time to move everything back.

Andrea's first stop was the hotel. She didn't want to be gone any longer than necessary; in fact, she would have preferred to stay home with Heather. She quickly changed her clothes, packed up her things, and had checked out of the hotel within fifteen minutes.

Her next stop was the mall. It would be chaos, being the day after Christmas, but there was something she needed to do. She marched into Helzberg's and had no difficulty choosing the perfect ring. It was simple and elegant and was made of eighteen-karat white gold. It had a three-quarter carat, princess cut center diamond and four accent diamonds, which totalled another three-quarter carats. She didn't bother to wait around for it to be gift-wrapped. The box would give away its contents regardless of the wrapping.

Now that she had the ring, she was nervous. Was it too soon? No. She wouldn't waste another minute of her time with Heather. They had wasted too much time already. Her drive over to the plant seemed to take forever. The ring in her pocket reminding her every second of who was waiting for her at home. She couldn't get this over with fast enough.

Although the plant was shut down for the holidays, she knew the people she needed to talk to would be in. They were always there. Shutdowns gave them the opportunity to get caught up without the interruption of day-to-day problems.

The silence in the plant was eerie. As she walked around looking for Carlos's boss, she greeted several maintenance workers who didn't have the luxury of enjoying the shutdown. They were busy repairing, cleaning, and maintaining equipment.

She spotted Mr. Adams sitting at his desk, surrounded by mountains of paperwork. She knocked on the door.

"Happy Holidays, sir," Andrea said nervously.

He greeted her with a warm smile and invited her to have a seat.

"What can I do for you, Andrea?"

"I was wondering if you had filled Mr. Greene's position yet?"

He smiled as if he had been keeping some big secret and said, "As a matter of fact, we haven't. In all honesty, we've been waiting for you to reconsider. Please tell me that you have."

Within minutes, Andrea was signing employment contracts, which had already been filled out in her name. They shook hands and she was on her way to her last stop before heading home.

Mr. Snickers, who normally would have given her grief for being late, seemed very understanding. She fed him quickly, cleaned his litter box, and gave him a few extra treats out of guilt. Tammy and Jamie would be home tomorrow; otherwise, she would have taken him home with her, so she wouldn't have to leave.

When Andrea returned home, after being gone for nearly four hours, she wanted to rush right in and give Heather the ring; it was burning a hole in her pocket. She was anxious, her heart was pounding, her stomach was in knots, but she wanted to wait for the right moment. It had to be romantic.

"Well?" Heather asked.

"I won't be travelling anymore. I took a job at the plant down here."

Heather rushed into her arms. "For real?"

"For real. Like it or not, you're stuck with me now."

"Oh, I like it! I like it a lot," she said as she showered Andrea with kisses.

"I redecorated your room while you were gone. I hope you don't mind," Heather said.

"Should I be afraid?" Andrea joked.

"Maybe," Heather replied nervously. What if Andrea wanted to keep her own space? She should have thought this through.

"Do I still have a bed on which I can ravish your body?"

"Yes."

"Then, that's all I need. Why do you look so scared?" She lifted Heather off the ground and carried her toward her room. "Show me."

Heather reached down, turned the doorknob and Andrea carried her into the room. She had no idea what Heather had meant when she said redecorated, but she was pleasantly surprised. She couldn't have been happier to see all of Heather's things in her room, although she did think they'd have to add some storage for Heather's clothes. For someone who wore a uniform to work, she certainly had an abundance of clothing.

"You're mad," Heather said when Andrea didn't say anything. "We should have talked about this first. I just ..."

Andrea lowered her to the ground and looked into her eyes.

"I'm not mad, Heather. Why would you think that? I'm actually very happy about it. It makes me feel a whole lot better about something I did."

"Andie, what did you do?" Heather asked accusingly, knowing Andrea's propensity to behave irrationally sometimes.

"Nothing bad, I promise."

"Tell me. Now I'm worried," Heather pleaded.

So much for the perfect romantic moment.

"This isn't how I had planned this but," Andrea said as she got down on one knee and reached into her pocket.

Heather looked at her in disbelief.

"You're not?" Heather said before covering the shocked expression on her face with her hand.

"I am," Andrea replied bravely. She opened the box, revealing the ring to Heather and said, "Heather, we've wasted enough time by not being true to our feelings. I don't want to waste another minute. Will you make me the happiest woman alive? Heather, will you marry me?"

Andrea held her breath and waited for Heather's response. Silent seconds passed that felt like an eternity.

"Yes, Andie! Yes, yes, yes!" She rushed into Andrea's arms and sobbed, unable to contain her happiness.

"Those are tears of joy, right? Because I made a promise to your mother."

"What?"

"Never mind. Let's see how this looks on your finger," Andrea suggested as she slipped the ring onto Heather's finger.

"It's beautiful, Andie. I love it. I love you."

"Would you like to join me on the bed and show me exactly how much you love me?" Andrea asked mischievously.

"Absolutely," Heather replied before playfully pushing Andrea back onto the bed and crawling on top of her.

She gazed down at Andie's gorgeous face for several seconds, and then ran her finger lightly over the scar on her forehead.

"I told you this needed stitches," she said before gently kissing it.

"I think it adds character," Andrea replied before pulling Heather's mouth to hers for a deep meaningful kiss.

Heather's hands struggled with Andie's clothes in their quest for flesh. She abruptly sat up, tugged at Andie's shirt and said, "Off." Andrea obediently removed her shirt and tried to help Heather out of hers.

"Don't," Heather said breathlessly. She looked down at Andie's legs, pointed at her jeans and said, "These … Gone!"

Andrea gave her a puzzled look but shimmied out of her jeans as directed. She tried again for Heather's shirt but Heather grabbed her wrists and pinned them over her head.

"No touching," Heather said with authority.

"Why not?" Andrea asked, completely amused at Heather's aggressiveness.

"Because you're like a teenager. I couldn't get past second base with you without making you come last night."

"I'm sorry," Andrea said in shame. She had tried so hard to maintain control of her body the night before, but nothing worked. She hoped that after a few times, the novelty would have worn off, but it hadn't.

"Don't be sorry, Andie," Heather replied and kissed her lightly on the lips. "I think it's sweet … but I will have my mouth on you before the day is through … one way or another, I'll find a way to make this work."

Andrea shuddered. Just thinking about it was driving her toward the edge. She felt like she was disappointing Heather, but she was helpless to control her reaction. Heather noticed Andrea struggling to maintain control. She quickly ran her hand down Andie's body, pausing when she met her hot, throbbing center.

"Andie, look at me," she said softly, her hand still resting gently and unmoving on her center.

Andrea opened her eyes and met Heather's gaze. Heather saw the look of determination in her eyes and ever so lightly, dipped her fingers into the waiting wetness. Andie took a deep breath and slammed her eyes shut.

"Heather, I …"

"It's okay, Andie. Let it go. Come for me," Heather replied encouragingly as she began to stroke the sensitive flesh.

"Heatherrrrr!!!" Andie was lost, floating somewhere over the bed as her orgasm consumed her. She felt as if she'd exploded into millions of tiny particles, which landed like a thin coat of dust on the bed. After what seemed to be an eternity, she was able to open her eyes, though her body remained lifeless and her head felt heavy and foggy.

"Hey," Heather said softly. "Welcome back."

"I … I …" Andrea tried to speak, but couldn't form a sentence.

Heather smiled and began teasing the sensitive flesh of Andrea's inner thighs with her fingers before she could protest. Andie whimpered and tried to wiggle away but she didn't have the strength.

Heather kissed her softly on the lips before trailing kisses down her chest, pausing briefly at each nipple before continuing her journey. She stopped just above Andie's left hip and ran her fingers over the tattoo teasingly before kissing it.

"Give me your hand," she said to Andie.

Andrea reached blindly for Heather's hand, entwining their fingers when they touched. Heather gently urged Andie's legs apart and began kissing her thighs, inhaling deeply, allowing Andie's scent to overtake her senses.

"Andie, look at me," she pleaded as she parted the soft swollen folds.

Andie's eyes were filled with desperation and need.

"I love you," Heather whispered before slipping her tongue into the dark, wet abyss. She used long, slow strokes, trying to keep Andie's orgasm from building too quickly.

Heather felt a twinge low in her belly. It was so unexpected she didn't realize she'd stopped moving until Andie squeezed her hand. She struggled to suppress her building orgasm as she devoured Andie with a newfound intensity. Andie's moans fuelled her own orgasm and she was powerless to fight it anymore.

She was afraid she'd come before Andie. How did this happen? It had never happened to her before.

"Andie, I'm going to … Oh, God! Andie, come with me."

She felt Andie's hand on the back of her head, guiding her to the place she needed her most. Seconds later, she felt Andie's muscles tighten.

"Jesus, Heather!" Andrea cried out.

Heather was lost, feasting feverishly on Andie's sweet juices, while trying to keep her own orgasm at bay. It was a futile attempt.

"Oh, God, Andie … Now!" she screamed.

Moment's later, Heather's listless body lay draped over Andie's. Her head was resting comfortably on Andie's stomach. Andrea ran her fingers through Heather's hair and sighed.

"That was …"

"Unexpected," Heather interrupted.

"I was going to say magical, but unexpected works. What happened, Heather?" she asked teasingly.

"Shut up, Andie."

Epilogue

▼

Mrs. Johnson went rushing into Heather's old bedroom, which Andrea was redecorating feverishly. Andrea inhaled deeply as the delicious aroma of Thanksgiving dinner drifted into the room in her wake.

"Andrea, it's time," Mrs. Johnson said calmly.

Andrea spun around, looked at her with an expression that resembled terror, dropped the paintbrush from her hand, and followed her mother-in-law out of the room.

"He's gorgeous," Tammy said, with Jamie standing next to her, as she peaked into his tiny little face with awe.

"Thank-you," Heather and Andrea replied in unison. They smiled proudly as their friends and family gathered with them in the small hospital room and took turns holding their newly born child.

"Have you decided on a name yet?" Mrs. Johnson asked curiously.

Heather looked to Andrea pensively and together they replied, "Donovan Andrew Johnson."

A gentle knock at the door caused them all to turn.

"Oh my gosh! Look how little he is!" Terri exclaimed in awe as she stood in the doorway with several packages in her hands.

"Hey, Ter," Andrea said. "Tell me all of those gifts aren't for him. You can't spoil him already."

"Of course I can. Not only am I his godmother, I'm also technically his aunt—double the reason to spoil him," Terri argued.

"Sorry I couldn't get here sooner. Trying to get a flight on Thanksgiving is a bit of a nightmare."

"We're glad you're here," Heather replied sincerely.

A short while later, Mrs. Johnson looked over at her daughter with concern and said, "We should probably get going and let you guys get some rest. Tammy, Jamie, and you too, Terri, are all welcome to come back to the house with us. There's an entire Thanksgiving dinner sitting there that hasn't been touched yet."

Hours later, after everyone else had left, Andrea sat in a chair next to Heather's bed holding baby Donovan in her arms and cried. She would make sure that he had the happiest, most wonderful childhood. She would protect him from the pain she endured growing up. She would teach him, encourage him, provide for him, and show him all of the love she missed out on in her life. Never would he question her love for him.

Heather quietly watched Andrea and wondered what she was thinking about. The love she felt for the two of them was immense. She felt as if she might burst with joy.

"I love you, Andie."

"Hey. How long have you been awake?" Andrea asked as she quickly wiped the tears from her face. She didn't want Heather to see her crying.

"Long enough," she replied to indicate that she had seen Andrea crying and whispering things to Donovan.

"Andie, I have no doubts that you will be a wonderful mother to our child," she added, almost as if she could read Andrea's mind.

"He's so beautiful, Heather. He looks just like you."

"That may be, but he will have your strength, your compassion, and your determination."

"Do you want to hold him for a while?"

"Only if I can hold the both of you," Heather replied and shifted over in the bed to make room for them.

Andrea carefully crawled in next to Heather and placed Donovan in her arms. She kissed them both softly, amazed at how much her life had changed in such a short time. "It's been quite a year," she said in astonishment.

"It certainly has," Heather agreed and rested her head on Andie's shoulder. "Did you ever think we'd be sitting here like this today?"

"I prayed for it everyday, but I didn't let myself believe it would happen."

"I hope you believe it now, because this little guy is very real, and ..." she smiled softly, "his diaper needs to be changed."

978-0-595-48667-0
0-595-48667-3

Printed in the United Kingdom by
Lightning Source UK Ltd., Milton Keynes
139575UK00001B/133/P